In Mem Murdered Churches

Marcel Proust
1921

NEWCOMB LIVRARIA
PRESS

Copyright © 2023 Tim Newcomb
All rights reserved.

All rights reserved under International and Pan-American Copyright Conventions. Published in the United States. The writings of Proust are now in the public domain in the European Union and the United States as they were printed in the late 19th and early 20th century.

Original translation by Newcomb Livraria Press 2023 from the original German 1st-edition printings using hybrid methods.

Quotations may be used for personal and commercial purposes.

No copyright claim is made with respect to public domain works. This edition contains minor editorial revisions in the translation of the original text. Cover design by Newcomb Livraria Press utilizing Canva Pro Content License Agreement Section 5 and Midjourney subscription. The information contained in this book is provided for educational and informational purposes only and is not intended as medical or psychological advice. The author, publisher, and translators assume no responsibility or liability for any errors or omissions in the content of this book or any actions taken by the reader based on the information provided.

Contents

In Memory **4**

Afterword by the Translator **64**

Timeline of Proust's Life and Works **71**

Glossary of Philosophic Terminology **74**

In Memory

I

Churches Saved
The Steeples of Caen.
The Cathedral of Lisieux

Days in the Cars

Leaving from... at a fairly late hour in the afternoon, I had no time to lose if I wanted to arrive before dark at my parents' home, about halfway between Lisieux and Louviers. To my right, to my left, in front of me, the car window, which I kept closed, put under glass the beautiful September day that, even in the open air, could only be seen through a kind of transparency. From as far away as they could see us, on the road where they stood bent over, rickety old houses ran to meet us, handing us a few fresh roses or proudly showing us the young hollyhock they had raised, which was already taller than them. Others came, leaning tenderly on a pear tree that their blind old age had the illusion of still supporting, and clutching it to their bruised hearts where it had immobilized and encrusted forever the sickly, passionate radiance of its branches. Soon, as the road turned and the embankment that flanked it on the right lowered, the plain of Caen came into view, without the city which, though included in the expanse I had before my eyes, could neither be seen nor guessed at, due to its remoteness. Only the two bell towers of Saint-Etienne rose up from the uniform level of the plain, as if lost in the open country. Soon we saw three of them, joined by the steeple of Saint-Pierre. Close together in a mountainous triple needle, they appeared like, often in Turner, the monastery or manor house that gives its name to the painting, but which, in the midst of the immense landscape of sky, vegetation and water, holds as little place, seems as episodic and momentary, as the rainbow, the five o'clock light, and the little peasant girl in the foreground, trotting along the path between her baskets. Minutes went by, we moved quickly, and yet the three steeples were always alone before us, like birds poised on the plain, motionless, and distinguishable in the sunlight. Then, with the distance tearing away like a mist that reveals in full detail a form invisible the moment before, the towers of the Trinité appeared, or rather a single tower, so exactly did it hide the other behind it. But then it moved aside, the other came forward and the two aligned. Finally, a lagging bell tower (Saint-Sauveur, I presume) came to stand in front of them in a bold volte face. Now, between the multiplied steeples, on whose slopes we could make out the light that we could see smiling from this distance, the city, obeying their impetus from below without being able to reach it, was developing the complicated but frank fugue of its roofs in vertical rises. I had asked the mechanic to stop for a moment in front of Saint-Etienne's steeples; but, remembering how long it had taken us to get close to them when they had seemed so close from the start, I pulled out my watch to see how many more minutes we'd take, when the car turned and stopped me at their foot. Having remained so long out of reach of the effort of our machine, which seemed to skate vainly along the road, always at the same distance from them, it was only in the last few seconds that the speed of all the time added up became appreciable. And then, giants, towering above us, they hurled themselves so roughly in front of us that we barely had time to stop and avoid colliding with the porch.

We continued on our way; we had long since left Caen, and the town, after accompanying us for a few seconds, had disappeared, as the two steeples of Saint-Etienne and Saint-Pierre, standing alone on the horizon watching us flee, still waved their sunlit summits in farewell. Occasionally, one faded away so that the other two could see us for a moment longer; soon, I saw only two. Then they turned one last time like two golden pivots, and disappeared from my view. Many a time since then, as the sun has set over the Caen plain, I've seen them again, sometimes from a great distance, like two flowers painted on the sky, above the low line of the fields; sometimes a little closer, already caught up by the steeple of Saint-Pierre, like the three maidens of a legend, abandoned in a solitude where darkness was beginning to fall ; and as I moved away I saw them timidly seeking their way and, after a few awkward attempts and stumbles of their noble silhouettes, clutching each other, slipping one behind the other, no longer making on the still pink sky but a single delicious and resigned black shape and fading into the night.

I was beginning to despair of arriving early enough in Lisieux to be with my parents that evening, who fortunately had not been informed of my arrival, when around the hour of sunset we started up a steep slope at the end of which, in the sun-blooded basin where we were speeding downhill, I saw Lisieux, which had preceded us, hastily raising and arranging its wounded houses, its tall chimneys stained crimson; In an instant, everything was back in its place, and when we stopped a few seconds later at the corner of Rue aux Fèvres, the old houses, with their fine ribbed wooden stalks that blossom into the heads of saints or demons at the windows, looked as if they hadn't moved since the 15th century. A machine accident forced us to stay until dusk in Lisieux; before leaving, I wanted to see again some of the foliage Ruskin spoke of on the cathedral façade, but the faint luminous lights that illuminated the city streets ceased on the square where Notre-Dame was almost plunged into darkness. I advanced, however, wanting at least to touch with my hand the illustrious stone grove, whose porch is planted and between whose two rows so nobly carved perhaps the bridal pomp of Henry II of England and Eleanor of Guyenne marched. But as I groped my way towards it, a sudden brightness flooded it; trunk by trunk, the pillars emerged from the night, vividly detaching, in full light against a background of shadow, the broad shape of their stone leaves. It was my mechanic, the ingenious Agostinelli, who, sending to the old sculptures the salvation of the present, whose light served only to better read the lessons of the past, directed successively on all parts of the porch, as I wanted to see them, the headlight of his automobile. And when I returned to the car, I saw a group of children who had been brought there by curiosity, and who, bending their heads towards the lighthouse, their curls pulsating in the supernatural light, were recomposing here, as if projected from the cathedral in a beam, the angelic figuration of a Nativity. By the time we left Lisieux, it was pitch-dark; my mechanic had donned a vast rubber mantle and donned a sort of hood which, hugging the fullness of his young, beardless face, made him look, as we plunged faster and faster into the night, like some pilgrim or rather some speed nun. From time to time - Saint Cecilia improvising on an even more immaterial instrument - he would touch the keyboard and play one of the stops on one of those organs hidden in the car, whose music, though continuous, we hardly notice except for those changes of register that are the changes of speed; music that is, so to speak, abstract, all symbol and number, and reminiscent of that harmony that spheres are said to produce when they rotate in the ether. But most of the time, he just held his wheel - his steering wheel - in his hand, similar to the crosses of consecration held by the apostles leaning against the choir columns in the Sainte-Chapelle in Paris, to the cross of St. Benedict, and in general to any stylization of the wheel in the art of the Middle Ages. He didn't appear to be using it, so much as he remained motionless, but held it as he would have done a symbol with which it was appropriate to be accompanied; thus the saints on the porches of cathedrals, one holding an anchor, another a wheel, a harp, a scythe, a grill, a hunting horn, paintbrushes. But if these attributes were generally intended to recall the art in which they excelled during their lifetime, they were also sometimes the image of the instrument by which they perished; may the steering wheel of the young mechanic driving me always remain the symbol of his talent rather than being the prefiguration of his torment! We had to stop in a village where, for a few moments, I was, for the locals, that "traveler" who no longer existed since the railroads and whom the automobile has resurrected, the one to whom the maid in the Flemish paintings pours out the stirrup, who we see in the landscapes of Cuyp, stopping to ask directions, as Ruskin puts it, of a passer-by whose appearance alone indicates that he is incapable of giving directions" and who, in La Fontaine's fables, rides into the sun and wind, covered in warm balandras at the onset of autumn, "when the traveler's precaution is good", - This "horseman" hardly exists today in reality, yet we still sometimes see him galloping at low tide along the seashore as the sun sets (no doubt brought out of the past by the evening shadows), making the seascape before our eyes a "navy" that we've never seen before, the eyes, a "marine" that he dates and signs, a little character who seems to have been added by Lingelbach, Wouwermans or Adrien Van de Velde, to satisfy the taste for anecdotes and figures of the wealthy Harlem merchants, lovers of painting, to a beach by Guillaume Van de Velde or Ruysdaël. But above all, the most precious thing that the automobile has given us about this traveler is the admirable independence that enabled him to leave at any time and stop wherever he pleased. I'm sure I'll be understood by all those who sometimes feel the irresistible desire to flee with the wind to the sea, where, instead of the inert village cobblestones battered by the storm, they'll be able to see the rising waves return blow for blow and rumor for rumor; all those, above all, who know what it can be like, on certain evenings, to be apprehensive about locking oneself in with one's sorrow for the whole night, all those who know what a joy it is, after struggling for a long time against one's anguish and as one began to climb towards one's room, stifling the beating of one's heart, to be able to stop and say to oneself: "Well! No, I won't get in; let's saddle up the horse, get the car ready", and all night long flee, leaving behind us the villages where our grief would have stifled us, where we guessed her under every little sleeping roof, as we sped past, unrecognized by her, out of her reach.

But the car had stopped at the corner of a sunken lane, in front of a door felted with blooming irises and roses. We had arrived at my parents' home. The mechanic blows his horn for the gardener to come and open the door, a sound we dislike for its shrillness and monotony, but which, like all matter, can become beautiful if impregnated with a feeling. In my parents' hearts, it resounded joyfully like an unexpected word... "It seems to me that I have heard... But then it can only be him!" They got up and lit a candle, shielding it from the wind of the door they had already opened in their impatience, while at the bottom of the park the trunk, whose now joyful, almost human sound they could no longer ignore, no longer ceased to sound its uniform call like the fixed idea of their coming joy, urgent and repeated like their growing anxiety. And I was thinking that in Tristan and Isolde (first in the second act, when Isolde waves her scarf like a signal, then in the third act, when the nave arrives) it is, the first time, the strident, indefinite and increasingly rapid repetition of two notes whose succession is sometimes produced by chance in the unorganized world of noises ; the second time, it is to the blowpipe of a poor shepherd, to the increasing intensity and insatiable monotony of his meagre song, that Wagner, in an apparent and genial abdication of his creative power, has entrusted the expression of the most prodigious expectation of bliss that has ever filled the human soul.

II

DAYS OF PILGRIMAGE

RUSKIN AT NOTRE-DAME D'AMIENS, ROUEN, ETC.

I would like to give the reader the desire and the means to spend a day in Amiens on a sort of Ruskin pilgrimage. There was no need to start by asking him to go to Florence or Venice, when Ruskin had written a whole book about Amiens. And, on the other hand, it seems to me that this is how the "cult of

Heroes" should be celebrated, I mean in spirit and in truth. We visit the place where a great man was born and the place where he died; but didn't he live in the places he admired most of all, whose very beauty we love in his books?

With a fetishism that is but illusion, we honor a tomb where only that which was not Ruskin himself remains, and we would not kneel before the stones of Amiens, from which he came to ask for his thoughts, and which still guard them, like the tomb in England where, of a poet whose body was consumed, only the heart remains - snatched from the flames by another poet?

No doubt the snobbery that makes everything it touches seem reasonable has not yet reached (for the French at least), and thus preserved from ridicule, these aesthetic strolls. Tell us you're going to Bayreuth to hear an opera by Wagner, or to Amsterdam to visit an exhibition of Flemish Primitives, and we'll be sorry we can't go with you. But if you admit that you're going to Pointe du Raz to see a storm, to Normandy to see apple trees in blossom, to Amiens to see a beloved statue by Ruskin, we can't help but smile. I hope you'll go to Amiens after reading this. When you work to please others you may not succeed, but the things you have done to please yourself always have a chance of interesting someone. It's impossible that there aren't people who take some pleasure in what has given me so much. For no one is original, and fortunately for the sympathy and understanding that are such great pleasures in life, it is from a universal fabric that our individualities are cut. If we knew how to analyze the soul as well as matter, we would see that, beneath the apparent diversity of spirits as well as that of things, there are few simple bodies and irreducible elements, and that in the composition of what we believe to be our personality, there are very common substances found almost everywhere in the Universe.

The indications that writers give us in their works about the places they have loved are often so vague that the pilgrimages we attempt there retain something uncertain and hesitant, like the fear of having been illusory. Like Edmond de Concourt's character looking for a grave with no cross to indicate it, we are reduced to making our devotions "haphazardly". You won't run the risk of having spent an afternoon there without having found him in the cathedral: he's come to pick you up at the station. He's going to find out not only how good you are at feeling the beauties of Notre-Dame, but how much time the time of the train you're planning to catch will allow you to devote to it. He won't just show you the way to the cathedral, but this way or that way, depending on whether you're in a hurry or not. And as he wants you to follow him in the free spirit that bodily satisfaction gives, perhaps also to show you that, like the saints to whom he prefers, he is not contemptuous of "honest" pleasure, before taking you to church, he will take you to the patissier. Stopping in Amiens with a thought of aesthetics, you are already welcome, for many do not do as you do: "The intelligent English traveler, in this fortunate century, knows that, halfway between Boulogne and Paris, there is an important railway station where his train, slowing its pace, rolls it with far more than the average number of noises and shocks expected at the entrance to every major French station, in order to recall by jolts the drowsy or distracted traveler to the feeling of his situation. He probably also remembers that at this stop in the middle of his journey, there is a well-served buffet where he has the privilege of a ten-minute break. He's not so clearly aware, however, that this ten-minute stop is less than a minute's walk from the main square of a city that was once the Venice of France. Leaving aside the islands of the lagoons, France's "Queen of the Waters" was about as wide as Venice itself, and crossed not by long currents of rising and falling tides, but by eleven beautiful trout streams... as wide as Isaac Walton's Dove, which come together again after they have swirled through its streets, are bordered as they descend towards the sands of Saint-Valéry, by aspen woods and bunches of poplars whose grace and cheerfulness seem to spring from each magnificent avenue like the image of the righteous man's life:

"Erit tanquam lignum quod plantatum est secus decursus aquarum."

But the Venice of Picardy owed its name not only to the beauty of its waterways, but also to the burden they carried. She was a worker, like the Adriatic princess, in gold and glass, stone, wood and ivory; she was as skilled as an Egyptian in weaving fine linen cloth, and combined the different colors in her needlework with the delicacy of the daughters of Judah. And of these, the fruits of her hands that celebrated her within her own gates, she also sent a portion to foreign nations, and her fame spread to all lands. Velvets of all colors, used to combat, as in Carpaccio, the carpets of the Turk and shine on the arabesque towers of Barbary. Why was this rainbow fountain spouting out here by the Somme? Why could a little French girl call herself the sister of Venice and the servant of Carthage and Tyre? The intelligent English traveller, obliged to buy his ham sandwich and be ready for "En voiture, messieurs", naturally has no time to waste on any of these questions. But that's talking too much about travelers for whom Amiens is just an important station to you, who have come to visit the cathedral and deserve to have your time put to better use; we're going to take you to Notre-Dame, but by which route?

"I've never been able to decide which is the best way to approach the cathedral for the first time. If you have plenty of leisure and the day is fine, the best thing to do would be to walk down the main street of the old town, cross the river and walk right out towards the limestone hill on which the citadel stands. From there you'll understand the real height of the towers and how much they rise above the rest of the town, then, on your way back, find your way down any side street; take whatever bridges you find; the more tortuous and dirty the streets, the better, and, whether you first reach the west facade or the apse, you'll find them worthy of all the trouble you've gone through to reach them.

"But if the day is dark, as it can sometimes be, even in France, or if you can't or won't walk, which can also happen because of all our athletic sports and lawntennis, or if really you have to go to Paris this afternoon and only want to see all you can in an hour or two, then assuming that, despite these weaknesses, you are still a nice enough sort of person for whom it is of some consequence which way he will arrive at a pretty thing and begin to look at it. I think the best thing to do then is to walk up the Rue des Trois-Cailloux. Stop for a while on the way to keep yourself in a good mood, and buy some tarts and sweets in one of the charming patissier stores on the left. Just after you've passed them, ask for the theater, and you'll go straight up to the south transept, which really does have something for everyone. Everyone has to love the airy embellishment of the spire above it, which seems to curve towards the west wind, though it doesn't; - at least its curvature is a long habit gradually contracted with increasing grace and submissiveness over these last three hundred years, - and arriving quite at the porch, everyone has to love the pretty little French Madonna that occupies the middle of it, with her head a little to one side, her nimbus to the side too, like a fetching hat. She is a Madonna of decadence, despite, or rather because of, her prettiness and her cheerful soubrette smile; she doesn't belong there either, for this is Saint Honoré's porch, not hers. Saint Honoré used to stand there, rough and gray, to receive you; now he's banished to the north porch, where no one ever enters. A long time ago, in the 14th century, when people first began to find Christianity too serious, made a happier faith for France and wanted to have a bright-eyed Madonna soubrette everywhere, leaving their own dark-eyed Joan of Arc to be burned as a witch; and since then things have gone their merry way, straight, "ça allait, ça ira", to the happiest days of the guillotine. But they still knew how to carve in the 14th century, and the Madonna and her lintel of hawthorn blossoms are worthy of your gaze, and even more so the equally delicate and calmer sculptures above, which tell the story of Saint

Honoré himself, little spoken of today in the Paris suburb that bears his name.

But you must be impatient to enter the cathedral. First, put a penny in the box of each of the beggars standing there. It's not your business whether they should be there or not, or whether they deserve the penny. Only know if you yourself deserve to have one to give, and give it nicely and not as if it burned your fingers."

It was this second, simpler route, and the one I suspect you'll prefer, that I followed, the first time I went to Amiens; and, as the south gate came into view, I saw before me, on the left, in the same place Ruskin indicates, the beggars he speaks of, so old indeed that they were perhaps still the same. Happy to be able to start following Ruskin's prescriptions so quickly, I went first and foremost to give them alms, with the illusion, in which entered that fetishism I was blaming earlier, of performing a high act of piety towards Ruskin. Associated with my charity, half in my offering, I thought I felt him leading my gesture. I knew, and at less expense, the state of mind of Frédéric Moreau in L'Education sentimentale, when on the boat, in front of Madame Arnoux, he extends his closed hand towards the harpist's cap and "opens it with modesty" to deposit a golden louis. It was not," says Flaubert, "vanity that impelled him to make this alms before her, but a thought of blessing in which he associated her, an almost religious movement of the heart."

Then, being too close to the portal to see the whole, I retraced my steps, and having reached the distance that seemed appropriate, only then did I look. It was a splendid day, and I had arrived at the hour when the sun makes its daily visit to the once-gilded Virgin, which today it only gilds during the moments when it restores to her, on the days when it shines, a different, fleeting and softer radiance. In fact, there's not a saint whom the sun doesn't visit, giving his shoulders a cloak of warmth and his forehead a halo of light. His day never ends without a tour of the immense cathedral. It was the hour of his visit to the Virgin, and it was to his momentary caress that she seemed to address her secular smile, the smile that Ruskin found, as you have seen, that of a soubrette to whom he prefers the queens, of a more naive and serious art, of the royal porch of Chartres. The reason I quoted the passage in which Ruskin explains this preference is that The Two Paths was published in 1850 and the Amiens Bible in 1885, the comparison of texts and dates shows how different the Amiens Bible is from these books, as we write so much about things we have studied so that we can talk about them (even supposing we have taken the trouble) instead of talking about things because we have studied them for a long time, to satisfy a disinterested taste, and without thinking that they might later become the subject of a book. I thought you'd like the Amiens Bible better, to feel that, in leafing through it, you were learning about the things Ruskin has always meditated on, those which express his thoughts most deeply; that the gift he was giving you was one of those most precious to those who love, and consists in objects which one has long used oneself, without any intention of ever giving them away, just for oneself. In writing his book, Ruskin didn't have to work for you, he only published his memory and opened his heart to you. I thought that the Golden Virgin would take on some importance in your eyes, when you saw that, nearly thirty years before the Amiens Bible, she had, in Ruskin's memory, her place where, when he needed to give his listeners an example, he knew how to find her, full of grace and charged with those serious thoughts to which he often gave rendezvous before her. Even then, she was one of those manifestations of beauty that not only gave his sensitive eyes a delight the like of which he never knew more vivid, but in which Nature, by giving him this aesthetic sense, had predestined him to seek, as in its most touching expression, what can be gathered from the earth of the True and the Divine. No doubt if, as has been said, in extreme old age, thought deserted Ruskin's head, like the mysterious bird that in a famous painting by Gustave Moreau does not wait for death to arrive before fleeing the house, - among the familiar forms that still crossed the old man's confused reverie without reflection being able to apply itself to them in passing, consider it probable that there was the Golden Virgin. Now maternal once more, as the Amiens sculptor depicted her, holding divine childhood in her arms, she must have been like the nurse who lets the one she has long cradled remain at her bedside. And, just as in the contact of familiar furniture, in the tasting of habitual dishes, old people experience, almost without knowing them, their last joys, discernible at least from the often fatal pain that would be caused by depriving them of them, believe that Ruskin felt an obscure pleasure in seeing a cast of the Golden Virgin, descended, by the invincible drive of time, from the heights of her thought and the predilections of her taste, into the depths of her unconscious life and the satisfactions of habit. As she is, with her distinctive smile that makes not only the Virgin a person, but the statue an individual work of art, she seems to reject this portal out of which she leans, to be no more than the museum to which we must go when we want to see her, as foreigners are obliged to go to the Louvre to see the Mona Lisa. But if cathedrals, as has been said, are the museums of religious art in the Middle Ages, they are living museums to which M. André Hallays would find nothing to object. They were not built to house works of art, but it is these works - however individual they may be - that were made for them and could not, without sacrilege (I'm talking here only about aesthetic sacrilege), be placed elsewhere. As she is, with her distinctive smile, how much I love the Golden Virgin, with her heavenly housewife smile; how much I love her welcome at this cathedral door, in her exquisitely simple hawthorn finery. Like the roses, lilies and fig trees on another porch, these sculpted hawthorns are still in bloom. But this medieval spring, so long prolonged, will not last forever, and the wind of the centuries has already stripped some of its stone roses in front of the church, as if on the solemn day of a perfume-free Corpus Christi. One day, no doubt, the smile of the Golden Virgin (which has already lasted longer than our faith) will cease to shed beauty for our children, as it did courage for our believing fathers, by crumbling the stones it gracefully pushes aside. I feel I was wrong to call it a work of art: a statue that is thus forever part of such and such a place on earth, of a certain city, that is to say, of a thing that bears a name like a person, that is an individual, the very same of which can never be found on the face of the continents, whose railway employees, in calling out its name to us, at the place where we inevitably had to come to find it, seem to be saying to us, without knowing it: "Love that which will never be seen twice" - there may be something less universal about such a statue than a work of art; at any rate, it holds us by a bond stronger than that of the work of art itself, one of those bonds that people and countries have to keep us. The Mona Lisa is Da Vinci's Mona Lisa. What does it matter to us (without wishing to displease Mr. Hallays) where she was born, or even that she is a naturalized French citizen? - She is something of an admirable "Sans-patrie". Wherever thought-laden gazes are cast upon her, she cannot be "uprooted". The same cannot be said of her smiling, sculpted sister (how much more inferior, need we say?) the Vierge Dorée. No doubt having emerged from the nearby quarries of Amiens, having made only one trip in her youth to the porch of Saint-Honoré, having remained there ever since, gradually tanned by the humid wind of the Venice of the North, which has curved the spire above her, and having looked for so many centuries at the inhabitants of this city, of which she is the oldest and most sedentary inhabitant, she is truly a native of Amiens. She's not a work of art. She is a beautiful friend whom we must leave in the melancholy provincial square from which no one has succeeded in taking her, and where, for eyes other than ours, she will continue to receive in her face the wind and sun of Amiens, to let the little sparrows land with a sure instinct for decoration in the hollow of her welcoming hand, or peck at the stone stamens of the ancient hawthorns that have made her a youthful adornment for so many centuries. In my room, a photograph of the Mona Lisa retains only the beauty of a masterpiece. Next to it, a photograph of the Golden Virgin takes on the melancholy of a memory. But let's not wait until the sun, with its innumerable rays and shadows resting on every relief of the stone, has ceased to silver the grey old age of the portal, at once sparkling and tarnished. It's been too long since we lost sight of Ruskin. We left him at the feet of this same Virgin, before whom his indulgence will have patiently waited for us to pay our own personal tribute. Let's enter the cathedral with him.

"We can enter no more advantageously than through this south door, for all cathedrals of any importance produce much the same effect when you enter through the west porch, but I know of no other that so reveals its nobility when viewed from the south transept. The rose opposite is exquisite and splendid, and the pillars on the lower sides of the transept form a marvellous whole with those of the choir and nave. From here, too, the apse shows its full height, revealing itself to you as you move from the transept into the central nave. Seen from the west end of the nave, on the other hand, an irreverent person might almost believe that it's not the apse that's high, but the nave that's narrow. If, on the other hand, you don't feel an admiration for the choir and the luminous circle that surrounds it, when you raise your eyes to it from the center of the cross, you don't need to keep traveling and looking for cathedrals, because the waiting room of any railway station is a place that suits you a thousand times better. But if, on the contrary, it astonishes and delights you first, then the better you get to know it, the more it will delight you, for it is not possible for the alliance of imagination and mathematics to accomplish anything more powerful and noble than this procession of stained glass windows, marrying stone to glass, nor anything that seems greater.

Whatever you see or are forced to leave aside, without having seen it, in Amiens, if the crushing responsibilities of your existence and the unavoidable necessities of a locomotion they precipitate leave you only a quarter of an hour - without being out of breath - for the contemplation of the capital of Picardy, give it entirely to the woodwork of the cathedral choir. You can see the portals, the ogival stained-glass windows and the roses just as well elsewhere as you can here, but you won't be able to see such a masterpiece of woodwork. It's flamboyant in its full development right at the end of the 15th century. You will see here the union of Flemish heaviness and the charming flame of the French style: carving the wood was the Picard's joy; in all I know I have never seen anything so marvellous carved from the trees of any country; it is a soft, young-grained wood; oak chosen and shaped for such work and which resonates now in the same way as it did four hundred years ago. Under the sculptor's hand, it seems to have molded like clay, bent like silk, sprouted like living branches, gushed like living flame... and soars, intertwines and branches into an enchanted glade, inextricable, imperishable, fuller of foliage than any forest and fuller of history than any book."

Now famous the world over, represented in museums by casts that the guardians won't let them touch, these stalls, themselves so old, so illustrious and so beautiful, continue to perform their modest stall functions in Amiens - which they have been doing for several centuries, to the great satisfaction of the people of Amiens - like those artists who, having achieved fame, nevertheless continue to hold down a small job or give lessons. Even before instructing souls, these functions consist in supporting bodies, and this is what they modestly do, folded down during each service and presenting their reverse side.

The ever-rubbed wood of these stalls has gradually taken on, or rather allowed to appear, that dark purple which is like their heart and which is preferred to everything else, until the eye, once enchanted by the colors of the paintings, can no longer look at them, which then seem quite crude. It's a kind of intoxication to taste, in the ever-increasing ardor of the wood, what is like the tree's overflowing sap over time. The naïveté of the characters sculpted here takes something twice natural from the material in which they live. And as for "these fruits, these flowers, these leaves and these branches", all motifs taken from local vegetation and carved by the Amiens sculptor from Amiens wood, the diversity of planes having resulted in different rubbing, we see admirable oppositions of tone, where the leaf stands out in a different color from the stem, reminiscent of the noble accents that M. Gallé has drawn from the harmonious heart of oak trees.

But it's time to move on to what Ruskin calls the Amiens Bible, in the Western Porch. Bible is taken here literally, not figuratively. The Amiens porch is not only, in the vague sense in which Victor Hugo would have taken it, a stone book, a stone Bible: it is "the Bible" in stone. Doubtless, before you know it, when you first see the western facade of Amiens, blue in the fog, dazzling in the morning, having absorbed the sun and richly golden in the afternoon, pink and already freshly nocturnal at sunset, at any of the hours that its bells ring in the sky, and that Claude Monet has fixed in sublime canvases where the life of this thing that men have made is revealed, but which nature has taken over by immersing it in itself, a cathedral, and whose life, like that of the earth in its double revolution, unfolds over the centuries, and on the other hand is renewed and completed each day, - then, freeing it from the changing colors with which nature envelops it, you feel before this facade a confused but powerful impression. Seeing this monumental, jagged swarm of human-sized figures in their stone stature, holding in their hands their cross, phylactery or sceptre, this world of saints, these generations of prophets, this retinue of apostles, this people of kings, this parade of sinners, this assembly of judges, this flight of angels, one beside the other, rising up to the sky, one above the other, standing by the door, looking down on the city from the top of the niches or from the edge of the galleries, higher still, receiving nothing but vague and dazzled glances from men at the foot of the towers and in the effluvium of the bells, no doubt in the heat of your emotion you feel that this giant, motionless and passionate ascent is a great thing. But a cathedral is not just a beauty to be felt. If it's no longer a teaching to be followed, it's still a book to be understood. The portal of a Gothic cathedral, and more specifically of Amiens, the Gothic cathedral par excellence, is the Bible. Before explaining it to you, I'd like to use a quote from Ruskin to make you understand that, whatever your beliefs, the Bible is something real, something current, and that we have to find in it something other than the flavor of its archaism and the entertainment of our curiosity.

"I, VIII, XII, XV. XIX, XXIII and XXIV Psalms, properly learned and believed, are enough for all personal guidance, have in them the law and prophecy of all just government, and every new discovery of natural science is anticipated in the CIV. Consider what other group of historical and didactic literature is as extensive as the Bible.

"Ask yourself if you can compare its table of contents, not to any other book, but to no other literature. Try, as far as it is possible for each of us - whether defender or opponent of the faith - to free our intelligence from the habit and association of moral sentiment based on the Bible, and ask yourself what literature could have taken its place or fulfilled its function, when even all the libraries of the universe would have remained untouched. I am no contemptor of secular literature, so little so that I do not believe any interpretation of Greek religion has ever been so affectionate, none of Roman religion so reverent as that which lies at the basis of my teaching of art and runs through the whole body of my works. But it was from the Bible that I learned Homer's symbols and Horace's faith. The duty imposed on me from my earliest youth, as I read every word of the Gospels and prophecies, to make it clear to myself that it was written by the hand of God, left me with the habit of a reverent attention which, later on, rendered many passages of secular authors, frivolous for irreligious readers, profoundly serious for me. How far my mind has been paralyzed by the faults and sorrows of my life; how far beyond my conjecture or confession; how short my knowledge of life is, compared to what I might have learned had I walked more faithfully in the light bestowed upon me, is beyond my conjecture or confession. But as I have never written for my own fame, I have been preserved from errors dangerous to others... and the fragmentary expressions... that I have been able to give... relate to a general system of interpretation of sacred literature, both classical and Christian.... That there is a classical sacred literature parallel to that of the Hebrews and merging with the symbolic legends of Christianity in the Middle Ages is a fact that appears most tenderly and strikingly in the independent yet similar influence of Virgil on Dante and Bishop Gawane Douglas. And the story of the Nemean lion vanquished with Athenaeus' help is the true root of the legend of St. Jerome's companion, conquered by the healing sweetness of the spirit of life. I call it a legend only. Whether Herakles ever killed or Saint Jerome ever cherished the wild or wounded creature, is of no importance to us. But the legend of Saint Jerome takes up the prophecy of the millennium and predicts with the Sibyl of Cumae, and with Isaiah, a day when the fear of man will cease to be hatred in lower creatures, and will extend over them as a blessing, when no more evil or destruction of any kind will be done in the whole expanse of the holy mountain and the peace of the earth will be delivered from its present sorrow, just as the present glorious animated universe emerged from the nascent desert whose depths were the dwelling places of dragons and whose mountains were domes of fire. That day no man knows, but the kingdom of God has already come for those who have torn from their own hearts what was rampant and inferior in nature and have learned to cherish what is lovely and human in the wandering children of clouds and fields."

And now perhaps you'd like to follow the summary I'll try to give you, according to Ruskin, of the Bible written on the western porch of Amiens.

In the middle is the statue of Christ, not figuratively, but literally, the cornerstone of the edifice. To his left (that is, to the right, for those of us looking out from the porch facing Christ, but we'll use the words left and right in relation to the statue of Christ) are six apostles: next to him Peter, then moving away from him, James the Greater, John, Matthew and Simon. To his right are Paul, then James the Bishop, Philip, Bartholomew, Thomas and Jude. Following the apostles are the four great prophets. After Simon, Isaiah and Jeremiah; after Jude, Ezekiel and Daniel; then, on the overmantels of the entire western façade come the twelve minor prophets; three on each of the four overmantels, and, starting with the overmantel furthest to the left: Hosea, Jael, Amos, Micah, Jonah, Obadiah, Nahum, Habakuk, Zephaniah, Haggai, Zechariah, Malachi. So the cathedral, always in the literal sense, rests on Christ, and on the prophets who foretold him and the apostles who proclaimed him. The prophets of Christ, not of God the Father:

"The voice of the whole monument is that which comes from heaven at the moment of the Transfiguration. This is my beloved son, listen to him. Also Moses, who was an apostle not of Christ but of God, and Elijah, who was a prophet not of Christ but of God, are not here. But, adds Ruskin, there's another great prophet who at first doesn't seem to be here. Will the people enter the temple singing: "Hosanna to the son of David", and see no image of his father? Did not Christ himself declare: "I am the root and the flowering of David", and the root would have no trace of the soil that nourished it? Not so; David and his son are together. David is the pedestal of the statue of Christ. He holds his scepter in his right hand, a phylactery in his left.

"Of the statue of Christ itself I will not speak, for no sculpture can or should satisfy the hope of a loving soul who has learned to believe in him. But at the time, it surpassed anything that had ever been achieved in sculpted tenderness. And she was known far and wide as: the beautiful God of Amiens. She was merely a sign, a symbol of the divine presence, not an idol in our sense of the word. And yet everyone conceived of her as the living Spirit, coming to welcome him at the door of the temple, the Word of life, the King of glory, the Lord of hosts. The "Lord of Virtues", Dominus Virtutum, is the best translation of the idea that the words of the 24th Psalm gave to an educated 13th-century disciple.

We can't dwell on each of the statues in the west porch. Ruskin will explain the meaning of the bas-reliefs below (two four-leaf bas-reliefs placed one below the other under each of them), those placed under each apostle representing: the upper bas-relief the virtue he taught or practiced, the lower the opposite vice. Below the prophets, the bas-reliefs depict their prophecies.

Beneath Saint Peter is Courage, with a leopard on its crest; below Courage, Cowardice is represented by a man who, frightened by an animal, drops his sword, while a bird continues to sing: "The coward does not have the courage of a thrush". Beneath Saint André is Patience, whose crest bears an ox (never backing down).

Below Patience is Wrath: a woman stabbing a man with a sword (Wrath, an essentially feminine vice that has nothing to do with indignation). Under Saint Jacques, Douceur, whose coat of arms bears a lamb, and Grossièreté: a woman kicking over her cupbearer, "the forms of the greatest French coarseness being in the gestures of the cancan".

Under St. John, Love, divine love, not human love: "I in them and you in me." His crest supports a tree with branches grafted into a felled trunk. "In those days the Messiah will be cut down, but not for himself. Below Love, Discord: a man and a woman quarrelling; she has dropped her distaff. Below Saint Matthew, Obedience. On its crest, a camel: "Today it is the most disobedient and unbearable beast," says Ruskin, "but the sculptor of the North knew little of its character. Since, despite everything, it spends its life in the most arduous service, I think he chose it as a symbol of passive obedience, which feels neither joy nor sympathy, as the horse does, and which, on the other hand, is not capable of doing harm like the ox. It is true that its bite is quite dangerous, but in Amiens it is highly probable that this was not known, even to the crusaders, who rode only their horses or nothing."

Below Obedience, Rebellion, a man snapping his finger at his bishop ("like Henry VIII at the Pope and the English and French onlookers at all the priests whoever they were").

Under St. Simon, Perseverance caresses a lion and holds its crown. "Hold fast what you have, so that no man may take your crown. Below, Atheism leaves its shoes at the church door. "In the 11th and 13th centuries, the foolish infidel was always depicted barefoot, with Christ having his feet wrapped in the preparation of the Gospel of Peace. "How beautiful are your feet in your shoes, O daughter of Prince!"

Below Saint Paul is Faith. Below Faith is Idolatry worshipping a monster. Below Saint James the Bishop is Hope holding a standard with a cross. Below Hope is Despair, stabbing itself.

Under St. Philip is Charity, giving her cloak to a naked beggar.

Under St. Bartholomew, Chastity with the phoenix, and below it, Lust, represented by a young man embracing a woman holding a scepter and a mirror. Under St. Thomas, Wisdom (an escutcheon with an edible root signifying temperance, the beginning of wisdom). Below her is Folly: the type used in all early psalters of a glutton armed with a club. "The fool has said in his heart: "There is no God; he devours my people like a piece of bread." (Psalm LIII). Under St. Jude, Humility wearing a crest with a dove, and Pride falling from a horse.

"Notice," says Ruskin, "that the apostles are all serene, almost all carrying a book, some a cross, but all the same message: 'Let there be peace in this house, and if the Son of Peace be here', etc., but the prophets all searching, or pensive, or tormented, or wondering, or praying, except Daniel. The most tormented of all is Isaiah. No scene of his martyrdom is depicted, but the bas-relief below him shows him catching a glimpse of the Lord in his temple, and yet he feels that his lips are impure. Jeremiah too carries his cross, but more serenely."

Unfortunately, we can't stop at the bas-reliefs which, below the prophets, depict the verses of their main prophecies: Ezekiel seated before two wheels, Daniel holding a book supported by lions, then seated at Balthazar's feast, the fig tree and vine without leaves, the sun and moon without light prophesied by Joel, Amos plucking the leaves of the fruitless vine to feed his sheep who find no grass, Jonah escaping from the waves, then seated under a calabash tree. Habakkuk, whom an angel holds by the hair, visiting Daniel, who caresses a young lion, Zephaniah's prophecies: the beasts of Nineveh, the Lord with a lantern in each hand, the hedgehog and the bittern, and so on.

I don't have time to take you to the two secondary doors of the western porch, that of the Virgin (which contains, in addition to the statue of the Virgin : to the left of the Virgin, those of the Angel Gabriel, the Virgin Annunciade, the Virgin Visitor, Saint Elizabeth, the Virgin presenting the Child to Saint Simeon, and to the right the three Magi, Herod, Solomon and the Queen of

Sheba, each statue having below it, like those in the main porch, bas-reliefs whose subject relates to it), - and that of Saint Firmin, which contains statues of Diocesan saints. It's no doubt because of this, because they are "friends of the people of Amiens", that the bas-reliefs below them represent the signs of the Zodiac and the labors of each month, bas-reliefs that Ruskin admires above all others. You will find casts of these bas-reliefs from the Porte Saint-Firmin in the Musée du Trocadéro, and in M. Mâle's book, charming comments on the local and climatic truth of these little genre scenes.

I have no business here," says Ruskin, "to study the art of these bas-reliefs. They were never intended to serve any other purpose than as guides to thought. And if the reader will simply let himself be led thus, he will be free to create for himself more beautiful pictures in his heart; and in any case, he will be able to hear the following truths affirmed by their whole.

"First of all, throughout this Sermon on the Mount of Amiens, Christ is never represented as the Crucified One, never for a moment awakens the thought of the dead Christ; but appears as the Incarnate Word - as the present Friend - as the Prince of Peace on earth - as the Eternal King in heaven. What his life is, what his commandments are, and what his judgment will be, we are taught, not what he once did, what he once suffered, but what he is doing now, and what he commands us to do. This is the pure, joyful and beautiful lesson that Christianity gives us; and the decadence of this faith, and the corruptions of a dissolving practice, can be attributed to the fact that we have accustomed ourselves to fix our gaze on the death of Christ, rather than on his life, and to substitute the meditation of his past suffering for that of our present duty.

"Then secondly, although Christ does not carry his cross, the afflicted prophets, the persecuted apostles, the martyred disciples, carry theirs. For if it is salutary for you to remember what your immortal Creator has done for you, it is no less salutary to remember what mortal men, our fellow creatures, have also done. You can, as you wish, deny Christ, renounce him, but you can only forget martyrdom; you cannot deny it. Every stone of this building has been cemented with his blood. So, keeping these things in your heart, turn now to the central statue of Christ; listen to his message and understand it. He holds the book of the Eternal Law in his left hand; with his right, he blesses, but blesses conditionally: "Do this and you will live" or rather in a stricter, more rigorous sense: "Be this and you will live": showing mercy is nothing, your soul must be full of mercy; being pure in action is nothing, you must be pure in your heart too.

"And with this word of the inabolic law:

"This if you do not, this if you are not, you will die". To die - whatever meaning you give to the word - totally and irrevocably.

"The gospel and its power are fully written in the great works of true believers: in Normandy and Sicily, on the islets of the rivers of France, at the river valleys of England, on the rocks of Orvieto, near the sands of the Arno. But the teaching that is at once the simplest and the most complete, that speaks with the most authority to the active mind of the North, is that which emerges from the first stones of Amiens.

"All human creatures, in all times and places of the world, who have warm affections, common sense and empire over themselves, have been and are naturally moral. The knowledge and command of these things has nothing to do with religion.

"But if, loving creatures who are like yourselves, you feel that you would love even more dearly creatures better than yourselves if they were revealed to you; if, striving with all your power to improve what is wrong near you and around you, you would like to think of the day when the Judge of all the earth will render all righteousness and the little hills will rejoice on all sides ; if, parting from the companions who have given you all the best joy you have ever had on earth, you wish ever again to meet their eyes and press their hands - where eyes will no longer be veiled, where hands will no longer fail ; if, preparing to lie under the grass in silence and solitude no longer seeing beauty, no longer feeling joy, you would care for the promise made to you of a time in which you would see the light of God and know the things you thirsted to know, and walk in the peace of eternal love - then the hope of these things for you is religion; their substance in your life is faith. And in their virtue we are promised that the kingdoms of this world will one day become the kingdoms of Our Lord and his Christ".

This is the end of the teaching that 13th-century men went to the cathedral to seek, and which, with an unnecessary and bizarre luxury, it continues to offer in a kind of open book, written in a solemn language where each character is a work of art, and which nobody understands any more. Giving it a less literally religious meaning than in the Middle Ages, or even just an aesthetic one, you have nevertheless been able to attach it to one of those feelings that appear to us beyond our life as the true reality, to one of "those stars to which it is appropriate to attach our chariot". Having misunderstood the significance of religious art in the Middle Ages, I said to myself, in my fervor for Ruskin: He will teach me, for isn't he too, in some respects at least, the truth? He will make my spirit enter where it had no access, for he is the door. He will purify me, for his inspiration is like the lily of the valley. He will intoxicate and enliven me, for he is the vine and the life. And indeed, I sensed that the mystical fragrance of the rosebushes of Sharon had not vanished forever, for it is still breathed, at least in his words. And now, the stones of Amiens have taken on for me the dignity of the stones of Venice, and the grandeur of the Bible, when it was still truth in the hearts of men and grave beauty in their works. The Amiens Bible was, in

Ruskin's mind, only the first book in a series entitled: Our Fathers Told Us; and indeed, if the old prophets of the Amiens porch were sacred to Ruskin, it was because the soul of thirteenth-century artists was still within them. Even before I knew whether I'd find it there, it was Ruskin's soul that I was going to look for, and which he imprinted as deeply on the stones of Amiens as those who sculpted them had imprinted theirs, for the words of genius can give things an immortal form just as well as the chisel. Literature, too, is a "sacrificial lamp" that burns itself out to enlighten its descendants. I was unconsciously complying with the spirit of the title: Our Fathers Told Us, by going to Amiens with these thoughts in mind, and with the desire to read Ruskin's Bible. For Ruskin, having believed in these men of old, because in them were faith and beauty, had found himself writing his own Bible, just as they, having believed in the prophets and apostles, had written theirs. For Ruskin, the statues of Jeremiah, Ezekiel and Amos were perhaps no longer in quite the same sense as they had been for the sculptors of yesteryear; they were at least the teaching work of great artists and men of faith, and the eternal meaning of unlearned prophecies. For us, if being the work of these artists and the meaning of these words is no longer enough to make them precious to us, let them at least be for us the things where Ruskin found this spirit, brother of his and father of ours. Before we came to the cathedral, was it not for us above all the one he had loved? and did we not feel that there were still Holy Scriptures, since we piously sought Truth in his books. And now, no matter how much we pause before the statues of Isaiah, Jeremiah, Ezekiel and Daniel, saying to ourselves: "These are the four great prophets, and after them the minor prophets, but there are only four great prophets", there's one more who isn't here, and yet we can't say he's absent, because we see him everywhere. It's Ruskin: if his statue isn't at the door of the cathedral, it's at the entrance to our hearts. This prophet has ceased to make his voice heard. But that's because he's finished saying all his words. It's up to the generations to take them up in chorus.

III

JOHN RUSKIN

Like "the Muses leaving Apollo their father to go and enlighten the world", one by one Ruskin's ideas had left the divine head that had borne them and, incarnated in living books, had gone to teach the peoples. Ruskin had withdrawn into the solitude where prophetic lives often end, until it pleases God to call back to himself the cenobite or ascetic whose superhuman task is finished. And we could only guess, through the veil stretched by pious hands, at the mystery that was being accomplished, the slow destruction of a perishable brain that had sheltered an immortal posterity.

Today, death has brought mankind into possession of the immense legacy Ruskin bequeathed it. For the man of genius can only give birth to works that will not die by creating them in the image not of the mortal being he is, but of the exemplar of humanity he carries within him. His thoughts are, as it were, on loan to him during his life, of which they are his companions. At death, they return to humanity and teach it. Such as this august and familiar dwelling in the rue de La Rochefoucauld, which was called Gustave Moreau's home for as long as he lived and which, since his death, has been called the Musée Gustave Moreau.

There has long been a John Ruskin Museum. Its catalog seems a compendium of all the arts and sciences. Photographs of master paintings stand side by side with mineral collections, as in Goethe's house. Like the Ruskin Museum, Ruskin's work is universal. He sought truth and found beauty even in chronological tables and social laws. But since logicians have given "Fine Arts" a definition that excludes mineralogy as well as political economy, it is only that part of Ruskin's work that concerns "Fine Arts" as they are generally understood, Ruskin as aesthetician and art critic, that I shall discuss here.

First of all, he was described as a realist. And, indeed, he often repeated that the artist should strive for the pure imitation of nature, "without rejecting anything, without despising anything, without choosing anything".

But he was also said to be an intellectualist, because he wrote that the best painting was the one that contained the highest thoughts. Speaking of the group of children in the foreground of Turner's Construction of Carthage, who are amused by sailing small boats, he concluded: "The exquisite choice of this episode, as a means of indicating the maritime genius from which the future greatness of the new city was to emerge, is a thought that would have lost nothing by being written down, that has nothing to do with the technicalities of art. A few words would have conveyed it to the mind as completely as the finest brushwork. Such a thought is something far superior to any art; it is poetry of the highest order." Similarly," adds Milsand quoting this passage, "in analyzing a Holy Family by Tintoretto, the feature Ruskin recognizes the great master for is a ruined wall and the beginnings of a building, by means of which the artist symbolically makes it clear that Christ's nativity was the end of the Jewish economy and the advent of the New Covenant. In a composition by the same Venetian, a Crucifixion, Ruskin sees a masterpiece of painting because the artist has managed, through a seemingly insignificant incident - the introduction of a donkey grazing palms in the background of Calvary, assert the profound idea that it was Jewish materialism, with its expectation of an all-temporal Messiah and the disappointment of its hopes upon entering Jerusalem, that had been the cause of the hatred unleashed against the Savior and, hence, of his death. "

It has been said that he suppressed the role of imagination in art by giving science too large a share. Didn't he say that "every class of rock, every variety of soil, every species of cloud must be studied and rendered with geological and meteorological accuracy?... Every geological formation has its essential features that belong to it alone, its determined fracture lines that give rise to constant forms in the soil and rocks, its particular plants, among which even more particular differences emerge as a result of varieties of elevation and temperature. The painter observes in the plant all its characteristics of form and color... grasps its lines of rigidity or repose... notices its local habits, its love or repugnance for this or that exposure, the conditions that make it live or that make it perish. He associates it... with all the features of the places it inhabits... He must trace the fine fissure and the descending curve and the undulating shadow of the crumbling ground, and render it with a finger as light as the touches of rain... A painting is admirable because of the number and importance of the information it gives us about realities".

On the other hand, it has been said that he ruined science by giving too much room to the imagination. And, indeed, one can't help but think of Bernardin de Saint-Pierre's naive finalism in saying that God divided melons into slices so that man could eat them more easily, when one reads pages like this: "God used color in his creation as an accompaniment to all that is pure and precious, while he reserved common hues for things of only material utility or for harmful things. Look at the neck of a dove and compare it to the grey back of a viper. The crocodile is gray, the innocent lizard is a splendid green."

If it has been said that he reduced art to being the mere vassal of science, as he pushed the theory of the work of art considered as information on the nature of things to the point of declaring that "a Turner discovers more about the nature of rocks than any academy will ever know", and that "a Tintoretto has only to let his hand go to reveal a multitude of truths about the play of muscles that will outwit all the anatomists of the world", it has also been said that he humiliated science before art.

Finally, it has been said that he was a pure aesthetician and that his only religion was that of Beauty, because he loved it all his life.

But, on the other hand, it has been said that he wasn't even an artist, because his appreciation of beauty was based on considerations that may have been superior, but were in any case alien to aesthetics. The first chapter of The Seven Lamps of Architecture prescribes that the architect use the most precious and durable materials, and derives this duty from the sacrifice of Jesus, and the permanent conditions of sacrifice pleasing to God, conditions which we have no reason to consider modified, since God has not expressly made known to us that they have been. And in Les Peintres modernes, to settle the question of who is right about the partisans of color and the adepts of chiaroscuro, here is one of his arguments: "Look at the whole of nature and generally compare rainbows, sunrises, roses, violets, butterflies, birds, goldfish, rubies, opals, corals, with alligators, hippos, sharks, slugs, bones, mold, fog and the mass of things that corrupt, that sting, that destroy, and then you'll feel how the question arises between the colorists and the chiaroscurists, which have nature and life on their side, which sin and death. "

And because so many contrary things were said about Ruskin, it was concluded that he was contradictory.

Of so many aspects of Ruskin's physiognomy, the one we are most familiar with, because it is the one of whom we possess, if we may so speak, the most studied and best-known portrait, the most striking and most widespread, is the Ruskin who knew only one religion all his life: that of Beauty.

That the adoration of Beauty was, indeed, the perpetual act of Ruskin's life, may be true to the letter; but I believe that the aim of this life, its deep, secret and constant intention, was something else, and if I say so, it is not to take issue with M. de la Sizeranne's system, but to prevent it being belittled in the minds of readers by a false, but natural and as it were inevitable, interpretation.

Not only was Ruskm's main religion religion tout court (and I'll come back to this point in a moment, as it dominates and characterizes his aesthetics), but, to confine ourselves for the moment to the "Religion of Beauty", our time should be warned that it can only pronounce these words, if it wants to make a fair allusion to Ruskin, by straightening the meaning that its aesthetic dilettantism is too inclined to give them. For an age, indeed, of dilettantes and aesthetes, a worshipper of Beauty is a man who, practicing no other cult than his own and recognizing no other god than her, would spend his life in the enjoyment that the voluptuous contemplation of works of art gives.

Yet, for reasons whose metaphysical investigation would go beyond a simple study of art, Beauty cannot be loved in a fruitful way if we love her only for the pleasures she gives. And, just as the search for happiness for its own sake only leads to boredom, and we have to look for something other than happiness to find it, so aesthetic pleasure is given to us by surcroit if we love Beauty for itself, as something real existing outside ourselves and infinitely more important than the joy it gives us. And, far from being a dilettante or an aesthete, Ruskin was precisely the opposite, one of those Carlyle-like men, warned by their genius of the vanity of all pleasure and, at the same time, of the presence beside them of an eternal reality, intuitively perceived by inspiration. Talent is given to them as a power to fix this reality to whose omnipotence and eternity, with enthusiasm and as if obeying a command of conscience, they dedicate their ephemeral lives to give it some value. Such men, attentive and anxious before the universe to be deciphered, are warned of the parts of reality on which their special gifts bestow a particular light, by a kind of demon that guides them, of voices they hear, the eternal inspiration of genial beings. Ruskin's special gift was a sense of beauty, in nature as in art. It was in Beauty that his temperament led him to seek reality, and his all-religious life was given a wholly aesthetic application. But the Beauty to which he devoted his life was not conceived by him as an object of enjoyment made to charm, but as a reality infinitely more important than life, for which he would have given his life. From this you will see Ruskin's aesthetics unfold. First of all, you'll understand how the years in which he became acquainted with a new school of architecture and painting could have been the key dates in his moral life. He will be able to speak of the years when the Gothic appeared to him with the same gravity, the same emotional return, the same serenity as a Christian speaks of the day when truth was revealed to him. The events of his life are intellectual, and the important dates are those when he penetrated a new art form, the year when he understood Abbeville, the year when he understood Rouen, the day when Titian's painting and the shadows in Titian's painting appeared to him as more noble than Rubens' painting, than the shadows in Rubens' painting.

You will then understand that, the poet being for Ruskin, as for Carlyle, a kind of scribe writing under the dictation of nature a more or less important part of its secret, the artist's first duty is to add nothing of his own to this divine message. From this height you will see the accusations of realism as well as intellectualism levelled at Ruskin vanish like clouds dragging themselves to earth. If these objections fail, it's because they don't aim high enough. There is an altitude error in these criticisms. The reality that the artist must record is both material and intellectual. Matter is real because it is an expression of the mind. As for mere appearance, no one has mocked more than Ruskin those who see its imitation as the goal of art. Whether the artist," he says, "has painted the hero or his horse, our enjoyment, in so far as it is caused by the perfection of the false semblance, is exactly the same. We only taste it when we forget the hero and his horse, and consider exclusively the artist's skill. You can consider tears as the effect of artifice or pain, one or the other as you wish; but both at the same time, never; if they fill you with wonder as a masterpiece of mimicry, they cannot touch you as a sign of suffering." If he attaches so much importance to the appearance of things, it's because it alone reveals their profound nature. M. de La Sizeranne has admirably translated a page in which Ruskin shows that the main lines of a tree show us which evil trees have tossed it aside, which winds have tormented it, and so on. The configuration of a thing is not only the image of its nature, it is the word of its destiny and the outline of its history.

Another consequence of this conception of art is this: if reality is one, and if the man of genius is the one who sees it, what does it matter what material he figures it in, be it paintings, statues, symphonies, laws, deeds? In his Heroes, Carlyle does not distinguish between Shakespeare and Cromwell, between Mohammed and Burns. Emerson counts Swedenborg and Montaigne among his representative men of humanity. The excess of the system is that, because of the unity of the reality translated, it does not differentiate deeply enough between the various modes of translation. Carlyle says it was inevitable that Boccaccio and Petrarch would be good diplomats, since they were good poets. Ruskin makes the same mistake when he says that "a painting is beautiful insofar as the ideas it translates into images are independent of the language of the images". It seems to me that, if Ruskin's system fails in any respect, it fails in this respect. For painting can only reach the one reality of things, and thus rival literature, if it is not literary.

If Ruskin has promulgated the artist's duty to scrupulously obey those "voices" of genius that tell him what is real and must be transcribed, it's because he himself has experienced what is true in inspiration, infallible in enthusiasm, fruitful in respect. However, although what arouses enthusiasm, what commands respect, what provokes inspiration is different for each, each ends up attributing to it a more particularly sacred character. It could be said that for Ruskin, this revelation, this guide, was the Bible.

Let's stop here, as if at a fixed point, at the center of gravity of Ruskin's aesthetics. This is how his religious feeling directed his aesthetic feeling. And first of all, to those who might believe that he altered it, that in the artistic appreciation of monuments, statues and paintings, he mixed in religious considerations that had no business there, let us reply that it was quite the opposite. The divine something that Ruskin sensed in the depths of his feeling for works of art was precisely that which was profound and original, and which imposed itself on his taste in an unalterable way. And the religious respect he brought to the expression of this feeling, his fear of subjecting it to the slightest distortion in translating it, prevented him, contrary to what has often been thought, from ever mixing his impressions of works of art with any artifice of reasoning that was foreign to them. As a result, those who see him as a moralist and an apostle who loved in art that which is not art, are as mistaken as those who, overlooking the profound essence of his aesthetic feeling, confuse it with a voluptuous dilettantism. As a result, his religious fervor, which had been a sign of his aesthetic sincerity, further strengthened it and protected it from any foreign influence. Whether this or that concept of his aesthetic supernaturalism is false is, in our opinion, of no importance. Anyone who has any notion of the laws of genius development knows that its strength is measured more by the strength of its beliefs than by what the object of those beliefs may have to satisfy common sense. But, since Ruskin's Christianity was the very essence of his intellectual nature, his artistic preferences, however profound, must have had some kinship with it. So, just as Turner's love of landscapes corresponded to Ruskin's love of nature, which gave him his greatest joys, so did the fundamentally Christian nature of his thought correspond to his permanent predilection, which dominated his entire life and work, for what might be called Christian art: the architecture and sculpture of the French Middle Ages, the architecture, sculpture and painting of the Italian Middle Ages. You don't need to look for traces of this in his life, you'll find the proof in his books. His experience was so vast, that often the most profound knowledge he demonstrates in one work is not used or mentioned, even by a mere allusion, in those other books where it belongs. He is so rich that he doesn't lend us his words; he gives them to us and never takes them back. You know, for example, that he wrote a book about Amiens Cathedral. You might conclude that this was the cathedral he loved best, or knew best. Yet in Seven Lamps of Architecture, where Rouen Cathedral is cited forty times as an example, Bayeux nine times, Amiens is not mentioned once. In Val d'Arno, he confesses that the church that gave him the deepest intoxication with the Gothic was Saint-Urbain de Troyes. Yet neither the Seven Lamps nor the Amiens Bible mention Saint-Urbain once. As for the absence of references to Amiens in the Seven Lamps, you may be thinking that he didn't know Amiens until the end of his life? He didn't. In 1859, in a lecture given at Kensington, he compares the Golden Virgin of Amiens at length with the less skilfully crafted but more deeply felt statues that seem to support the western porch of Chartres. And yet, in the Bible d'Amiens, where we might believe that he has brought together everything he thought about Amiens, not once, in the pages where he speaks of the Vierge Dorée, does he allude to the Chartres statues. Such is the infinite richness of his love and knowledge. Usually, with a writer, the return to certain favorite examples, if not even the repetition of certain developments, reminds you that you are dealing with a man who has had a certain life, such knowledge that takes the place of such other knowledge, a limited experience from which he draws all the profit he can. Just by consulting the indexes to Ruskin's various works, the perpetual novelty of the works cited, even more the disdain for a piece of knowledge he used once and, very often, abandoned forever, give the idea of something more than human, or rather the impression that each book is by a new man with a different knowledge, not the same experience, a different life.

It was the charming game of his inexhaustible wealth to draw ever-new treasures from the marvellous jewel cases of his memory: one day the precious rose of Amiens, another the golden lace of the Abbeville porch, to marry them with the dazzling jewels of Italy.

He could, in fact, move from one country to another, for the same soul he had worshipped in the stones of Pisa was also the one who had given the stones of Chartres their immortal form. The unity of Christian art in the Middle Ages, from the banks of the Somme to the shores of the Arno, was felt by no one like him, and he realized in our hearts the dream of the great popes of the Middle Ages: "Christian Europe". If, as has been said, his name is to remain attached to Pre-Raphaelism, we should understand it not as post-Turner, but pre-Raphael. We can forget today the services he rendered to Hunt, to Rossetti, to Millais; but what he did for Giotto, for Carpaccio, for Bellini, we cannot. His divine work was not to raise the living, but to resurrect the dead.

Doesn't this unity of Christian art of the Middle Ages appear at every moment in the perspective of these pages where his imagination here and there illuminates the stones of France with a magical reflection of Italy? Earlier in Pleasures of England, we saw him compare Giotto's Charité d'Amiens with the Charité d'Amiens. See him, in Natur of Gothic, compare the way flames are treated in Italian Gothic and French Gothic, of which the porch of Saint-Maclou in Rouen is taken as an example. And, in Les Sept Lampes de l'Architecture (Seven Lamps of

Architecture), in reference to this same porch, you can still see a touch of Italian color playing on its gray stones.

"The bas-reliefs on the tympanum of the portal of Saint-Maclou, Rouen, represent the Last Judgment, and the Inferno section is treated with a power at once terrible and grotesque, which I could not better define as a blend of the spirits of Orcagna and Hogarth. The demons are perhaps even more frightening than Orcagna's; and in certain expressions of degraded humanity, in its supreme despair, the English painter is at least equaled. No less fierce is the imagination that expresses fury and fear, even in the way the figures are placed. An evil angel, swinging on his wing, leads the troops of the damned out of the Judgment Seat; they are pressed by him so furiously, that they are taken not simply to the extreme limit of this scene which the sculptor has enclosed elsewhere inside the tympanum, but out of the tympanum and into the niches of the vault ; while the flames that follow them, activated, as it seems, by the movement of the angels' wings, also erupt into the niches and gush through their networks, the three lowest niches being depicted as all ablaze, while, instead of their usual vaulted, ribbed canopy, there's a demon on the roof of each, with its wings folded, scowling out of the black shadow. "

This parallelism of different kinds of art and different countries was not the deepest he had to stop at. In pagan and Christian symbols, the identity of certain religious ideas must have struck him. Ary Renan has remarked in depth on how much of Christ there already is in Gustave Moreau's Prométhée. Ruskin, whose devotion to Christian art never made him contemptuous of paganism, compared the lion of St. Jerome to the lion of Nemea, Virgil to Dante, Samson to Hercules, Theseus to the Black Prince, and the predictions of Isaiah to those of the Sybil of Cumae. There is certainly no reason to compare Ruskin to Gustave Moreau, but it can be said that a natural tendency, developed by frequenting the Primitives, had led them both to proscribe the expression of violent feelings in art, and, insofar as it had been applied to the study of symbols, to a certain fetishism in the adoration of symbols themselves, a fetishism that was in any case not very dangerous for minds so deeply attached to symbolized sentiment that they could pass from one symbol to another without being stopped by purely surface diversities. As for the systematic prohibition of the expression of violent emotions in art, the principle that Mr. Ary Renan has called the Principle of Beautiful Inertia, where better to find it defined than in the pages of "Rapports de Michel-Ange et du Tintoret"? As for the somewhat exclusive adoration of symbols, wasn't the study of Italian and French medieval art bound to lead to this? And since, beneath the work of art, it was the soul of a time that he was seeking, the resemblance of these symbols from the Chartres portal to the frescoes of Pisa was bound to strike him as proof of the typical originality of the spirit that animated artists at the time, and their differences as a testimony to its variety. In anyone else, aesthetic sensations would have risked being dampened by reasoning. But with him, everything was love, and iconography, as he understood it, would have been better called iconolatry. At this point, moreover, art criticism gives way to something greater perhaps; it has almost the procedures of science, it contributes to history. The appearance of a new attribute on the porches of cathedrals warns us of no less profound changes in the history, not only of art, but of civilization, than those announced to geologists by the appearance of a new species on earth. The stone carved by nature is no more instructive than the stone carved by the artist, and we derive no greater benefit from that which preserves for us an ancient monster than from that which shows us a new god.

The drawings that accompany Ruskin's writings are highly significant in this respect. In the same plate, you can see the same architectural motif, as treated in Lisieux, Bayeux, Verona and Padua, as if they were varieties of the same species of butterfly under different skies. But these stones he loved so much never became abstract examples for him. On each stone you see the hue of the hour united with the color of the centuries. Running to Saint-Wulfram d'Abbeville," he tells us, "before the sun has left the towers, was always for me one of those joys for which one must cherish the past until the end." He went even further, not separating the cathedrals from the backdrop of rivers and valleys, where they appear to the approaching traveller as in a primitive painting. One of his most instructive drawings in this respect is the one reproduced in the second engraving of Our Father have told us, entitled: Amiens, le jour des Trépassés. In the towns of Amiens, Abbeville, Beauvais and Rouen, all of which Ruskin's stay in France was dedicated to, he spent his time drawing, sometimes in church ("without being bothered by the sacristan"), sometimes in the open air. And they must have been very charming temporary colonies in these cities, this troop of draughtsmen and engravers that he took with him, as Plato shows us the sophists following Protagoras from town to town, similar also to the swallows, in imitation of which they preferred to stop at the old roofs, the ancient towers of cathedrals. Perhaps we could still find some of those disciples of Ruskin who accompanied him to the banks of this Somme evangelized anew, as if the times of Saint Firmin and Saint Salve had returned, and who, while the new apostle spoke, explaining Amiens like a Bible, took instead of notes, drawings, graceful notes whose file is undoubtedly in an English museum room, and where I imagine that reality must be slightly arranged, in the taste of Viollet-le-Duc. The engraving Amiens, le jour des Trépassés, seems to lie a little for beauty. Is it perspective alone that brings the cathedral and the church of Saint-Leu so close to the banks of an enlarged Somme? It's true that Ruskin could answer us with Turner's own words, quoted in Eagles Nest and translated by M. de La Sizeranne: "Turner, in the first period of his life, was sometimes in a good humour and showed people what he was doing. One day he was drawing Plymouth harbor and some ships, a mile or two away, seen against the current. Having shown this drawing to a naval officer, the latter observed with surprise and objected with very understandable indignation that ships of the line had no gun ports. No," said Turner, "certainly not. If you climb Mount Edgecumbe and look at the ships against the light of the setting sun, you'll see that you can't see the gun ports. - Well," said the still indignant officer, "you know there are ports there? - Yes," said Turner, "I know from the rest, but my business is to draw what I see, not what I know."

If, being in Amiens, you go in the direction of the abattoir, you will have a view not unlike that of the engraving. You'll see the distance arranging, in an artist's mendacious and happy way, monuments, which will resume, if you then move closer, their primitive position, quite different; you'll see him, for example, inscribing in the facade of the cathedral the figure of one of the city's water machines and making plane geometry with geometry in space. If, however, you find this landscape, tastefully composed through perspective, a little different from the one depicted in Ruskin's drawing, you can blame it mainly on the changes in the city's appearance brought about by the almost twenty years that have passed since Ruskin stayed there, and, as he said of another site he loved, "all the embellishments that have occurred since I composed and meditated there".

But at least this engraving from the Amiens Bible will have associated the banks of the Somme and the cathedral in your memory more than your vision could probably have done at any point in the city. It will prove to you better than anything I could have said, that Ruskin did not separate the beauty of cathedrals from the charm of the countries from which they sprang, and that everyone who visits them still tastes in the particular poetry of the country and the hazy or golden memory of the afternoon he spent there. Not only is the first chapter of the Amiens Bible called Au bord des courants d'eau vive, but the book Ruskin planned to write about Chartres Cathedral was to be entitled Les Sources de l'Eure. So it wasn't just in his drawings that he set churches beside rivers and associated the grandeur of Gothic cathedrals with the grace of French sites. And the individual charm that is the charm of a country, we would feel more keenly if we didn't have at our disposal the seven-league boots that are the great expresses, and if, as in the past, to reach a corner of the world we were obliged to cross countryside more and more similar to that to which we tend, like zones of graduated harmony which, by making it less easily penetrable by what is different from it, by protecting it gently and mysteriously with fraternal resemblances, not only envelop it in nature, but also prepare it in our minds.

Ruskin's studies of Christian art were, for him, the verification and counter-proof of his ideas on Christianity and of other ideas that we have not been able to indicate here, and of which we will shortly let Ruskin himself define the most famous: his abhorrence of machinism and industrial art. "All beautiful things were made, when the men of the Middle Ages believed the pure, joyful and beautiful lesson of Christianity." And then he saw art decline with faith, skill take the place of feeling. Seeing the power to realize beauty that was the privilege of the ages of faith, his belief in the goodness of faith must have been strengthened. Each volume of his last work: Our Father have told us (the first alone is written) was to comprise four chapters, the last of which was devoted to the masterpiece that was the flowering of the faith whose study was the subject of the first three chapters. In this way, Christianity, which had cradled Ruskin's aesthetic feelings, received its supreme consecration. And after having mocked his Protestant reader "who should understand that the worship of no Lady has ever been pernicious to mankind", when leading her before the statue of the Madonna, or before the statue of Saint Honoré, after having deplored the fact that so little was said about this saint "in the suburb of Paris that bears his name", he could have said, as at the end of Val d'Arno:

"If you want to fix your minds on what is required of human life by the one who gave it: 'He has shown you, man, what is good, and what does the Lord require of you but to act justly and love mercy, to walk humbly with your God?' you will find that such obedience is always rewarded with a blessing." If you turn your thoughts back to the state of the forgotten multitudes who toiled in silence and worshipped humbly, as the snows of Christendom brought back the memory of Christ's birth or the sun of his spring the memory of his resurrection, you will know that the promise of the angels of Bethlehem has been literally fulfilled, and you will pray that your English fields, joyfully, like the banks of the Arno, may yet dedicate their pure lilies to Saint Mary of the Flowers."

Finally, Ruskin's medieval studies confirmed, along with his belief in the goodness of faith, his belief in the necessity of free, joyful and personal work, without the intervention of machinism. To make this clear to you, it's best to transcribe here one of Ruskin's most characteristic pages. He's talking about a small figure, just a few centimetres tall, lost amid hundreds of tiny figures, at the Portal des Librairies, in Rouen Cathedral,

"The companion is bored and embarrassed in his mischief, and his hand is pressed hard against the bone of his cheek and the flesh of the cheek wrinkled below the eye by the pressure. The whole may seem terribly rudimentary, if compared with delicate engravings; but, considering it as merely to fill a gap in the exterior of a cathedral door and as any one of three hundred or more analogous figures, it testifies to the noblest vitality in the art of the age.

"We have some work to do to earn our bread, and it must be done with ardor; other work to do for our joy, and that one must be done with heart; neither of these must be done half-heartedly or by means of expedients, but with will ; and that which is not worthy of this effort must not be done at all; perhaps all that we have to do here below has no other object than to exercise the heart and the will, and is in itself useless; but in any case, however little it may be, we can dispense with it if it is not worthy that we put our hands and our heart into it. It does not befit our immortality to resort to means that contrast with its authority, nor to suffer an instrument it does not need to come between it and the things it governs. There is enough daydreaming, enough coarseness and sensuality in human existence, without changing its few shining moments into a mechanism; and, since our life - to put things at their best - must be but a vapor that appears for a time, then vanishes, let it at least appear as a cloud in the height of heaven and not as the thick darkness that gathers around the blast of the furnace and the revolutions of the wheel."

I confess that when I reread this page at the time of Ruskin's death, I was seized with the desire to see the little man of whom he speaks. And I went to Rouen as if obeying a testamentary thought, and as if Ruskin in dying had somehow entrusted to his readers the poor creature to whom he had, by speaking of her, given back life, and who had just, without knowing it, lost forever the one who had done as much for her as her first sculptor. But when I arrived near the immense cathedral and in front of the door where the saints basked in the sun, higher up, from the galleries where the kings shone to those supreme altitudes of stone that I thought uninhabited and where, here, a sculpted hermit lived isolated, letting the birds stay on his forehead, while there, a cenacle of apostles listened to the message of an angel who landed beside them, folding his wings, under a flock of pigeons opening theirs, and not far from a figure who, receiving a child on his back, turned his head with a brusque, secular gesture ; when I saw, lined up in front of its porches or leaning over the balconies of its towers, all the stone hosts of the mystical city breathing in the sun or the morning shade, I realized that it would be impossible to find among this superhuman people a figure just a few centimetres tall.

Nevertheless, I went to the portal of the Librairies. But how could I recognize the small figure among hundreds of others? Suddenly, a talented young sculptor, Mrs. L. Yeatmen, said to me: "Here's one that looks like her. We look a little lower, and... there it is. It's not even ten centimetres long. It's crumbled, and yet it's still his gaze, the stone retaining the hole that raises the pupil and gives it that expression that made me recognize it. The artist who died centuries ago left here, among thousands of others, this little person who dies a little every day, and who had been dead for a long time, lost among the crowd of others, forever. But he had put it there. One day, a man for whom there is no death, for whom there is no material infinity, no oblivion, a man who, throwing away the nothingness that oppresses us in order to reach the goals that dominate his life, so numerous that he won't be able to reach them all while we seem to lack them, this man came, and, in these waves of stone where each jagged foam seemed to resemble the others, seeing there all the laws of life, all the thoughts of the soul, naming them by their name, he said: "See, it's this, it's that. " Such as on the Day of Judgment, which not far off is figurative, he sounds in his words like the archangel's trumpet and says: "Those who have lived will live; matter is nothing." And, indeed, like the dead that not far away the tympanum figures, awakened to the archangel's trumpet, lifted up, having regained their form, recognizable, alive, behold, the little figure has lived again and regained its gaze, and the Judge has said, "You have lived, you will live." For him, he is not an immortal Judge, his body will die; but what does it matter! as if he were not to die he accomplishes his immortal task, not caring about the greatness of the thing that occupies his time and, having only a human life to live, he spends several days in front of one of the ten thousand figures in a church. He drew it. For him, it corresponded to the ideas that stirred his brain, unconcerned about the prospect of old age. He drew it, he talked about it. And the harmless, monstrous little figure was resurrected, against all hope, from that death which seems more total than the others, which is disappearance in the midst of the infinity of numbers and the levelling of resemblances, but from which genius soon pulls us too. Finding her there, you can't help but be touched. She seems to live and look, or rather to have been caught by death in her very gaze, like the Pompeians whose gesture remains interrupted. And it is indeed one of the sculptor's thoughts that has been captured here in his gesture by the immobility of the stone. I was touched to find it there; nothing dies from what has lived, no more the sculptor's thought than Ruskin's thought.

Encountering it there, necessary to Ruskin who, among so few engravings illustrating his book, dedicated one to it because it was for him a current and lasting part of his thought, and pleasing to us because his thought is necessary to us, a guide to ours which has encountered it on its way, we felt ourselves to be in a state of mind closer to that of the artists who sculpted the Last Judgement on the tympanums, and who believed that the individual, that which is most particular in a person, in an intention, does not die, remains in God's memory and will be resurrected. Who's right, the gravedigger or Hamlet, when the former sees only a skull while the latter remembers a fantasy? Science may say: the gravedigger; but it has counted without Shakespeare, who will make the memory of this fantasy last beyond the dust of the skull. At the angel's call, every dead person is found to have remained there, in its place, when we thought it had long since turned to dust. At Ruskin's call, we see the tiniest figure framing a tiny quatrefoil resurrected in its form, looking at us with the same gaze that seems to fit only a millimeter of stone. No doubt, poor little monster, I wouldn't have been strong enough, among the billions of stones of the cities, to find you, to free your face, to find your personality, to call you, to bring you back to life. But it's not that the infinite, the numbers, the nothingness that oppress us are very strong; it's that my thinking isn't very strong. Certainly, there was nothing really beautiful about you. Your poor face, which I would never have noticed, doesn't have a very interesting expression, although of course it has, like every other person, an expression that no other person ever had. But, since you lived long enough to keep looking with that same oblique gaze, for Ruskin to notice you and, after he had said your name, for his reader to recognize you, are you alive long enough now, are you loved long enough? And one can't help thinking of you with tenderness, even though you don't look good, but because you're a living creature, because for so many centuries you died without hope of resurrection, and because you've risen again. And one of these days perhaps someone else will come and find you at your gate, gazing with tenderness at your wicked, oblique resurrected figure, because what has come out of one thought can alone one day fix another thought which in turn has fascinated ours. You were right to remain there, unregarded, crumbling. You could expect nothing from matter, where you were nothing but nothingness. But the little ones have nothing to fear, nor the dead. For, sometimes, the Spirit visits the earth; as it passes, the dead rise up, and the little forgotten figures find their gaze again and stare into the eyes of the living, who, for their sake, abandon the living who do not live, and go to seek life only where the Spirit has shown it to them, in stones that are already dust and are still thought.

He who enveloped the old cathedrals with more love and more joy than the sun can bestow on them when it adds its fleeting smile to their age-old beauty cannot, to hear him well, have been mistaken. The spirit world is like the physical universe, where the height of a jet of water cannot exceed the height of the place from which it first descended. Great literary beauties correspond to something, and it is perhaps enthusiasm in art that is the criterion of truth. Assuming that Ruskin has sometimes erred, as a critic, in accurately assessing the value of a work, the beauty of his erroneous judgment is often more interesting than that of the work being judged, and corresponds to something which, for being other than it, is no less precious. That Ruskin is wrong when he says that the Beau Dieu d'Amiens "surpassed in sculpted tenderness what had hitherto been achieved, although any representation of Christ must eternally disappoint the hope that every loving soul has placed in him", and that it is M. Huysmans who is right when he calls this same Dieu d'Amiens a "sheep-faced bellicose", is what we do not believe, but it is what it does not matter to know. Whether or not the Handsome God of Amiens is what Ruskin believed is irrelevant to us. As Buffon said that "all the intellectual beauties that are to be found in it (in a beautiful style), all the relationships of which it is composed, are as many truths as useful and perhaps more valuable to the public mind than those that can make up the substance of the subject", the truths of which the beauty of the pages of the Bible on the Beau Dieu d'Amiens is composed have a value independent of the beauty of this statue, and Ruskin would not have found them if he had spoken of them with disdain, for enthusiasm alone could have given him the power to discover them.

How far this marvellous soul has faithfully reflected the universe, and in what touching and tempting forms the lie may have crept despite everything into the bosom of its intellectual sincerity, is what we may never be given to know, and what in any case we cannot seek here. Be that as it may, he was one of those "geniuses" that even those of us who were born with the gifts of fairies need to be initiated into the knowledge and love of a new part of Beauty. Many of the words our contemporaries use to exchange thoughts bear his imprint, just as we see the effigy of the day's ruler on coins. Dead, he continues to enlighten us, like those extinguished stars whose light still reaches us, and we can say of him what he said at Turner's death: "It is through these eyes, closed forever at the bottom of the tomb, that generations yet unborn will see nature."

"In what magnificent and tempting forms could the lie have crept to the bosom of his intellectual sincerity..." Here's what I meant: there's a kind of idolatry that no one defined better than

Ruskin in a page from Lectures on Art: "It has been, I think, not unmixed with good, no doubt, for the greatest evils bring some good in their reflux, it has been, I think, the really harmful role of art, to help what, in pagans and Christians alike - whether it be the mirage of words, colors or beautiful forms, - really must, in the deepest sense of the word, be called idolatry, that is, serving with the best of our hearts and minds some dear or sad image we've created for ourselves, while we disobey the present call of the Master, who is not dead, who is not faltering at this moment under his cross, but commands us to bear ours. Yet it seems that at the root of Ruskin's work, at the root of his talent, lies precisely this idolatry. Undoubtedly, he never allowed it to completely cover, - even to embellish, - immobilize, paralyze and ultimately kill, his intellectual and moral sincerity. In every line of his work, as in every moment of his life, we sense the need for sincerity that fights against idolatry, that proclaims its vanity, that humbles beauty in the face of duty, however unsightly. I won't take examples from his life (which is not like the life of a Racine, a Tolstoy or a Maeterlinck, aesthetic first and moral second, but in which morality asserted its rights from the outset within aesthetics itself - without perhaps ever freeing itself from it as completely as in the lives of the Masters I've just mentioned). I don't need to go through the stages, from his first qualms about drinking tea while looking at Titian paintings, to the moment when, having spent the five million his father had left him on philanthropic and social works, he decided to sell his Turners. But there is a dilettantism more interior than the dilettantism of action (which he had triumphed over) and the real duel between his idolatry and his sincerity was played out not at certain hours of his life, not in certain pages of his books, but at every minute, in those deep, secret regions almost unknown to us, secret, almost unknown to ourselves, where our personality receives images from the imagination, ideas from the intelligence, words from the memory, asserts itself in the incessant choice it makes of them, and incessantly plays out the fate of our spiritual and moral life. In these regions, I have the impression that the sin of idolatry was constantly being committed by Ruskin. And at the very moment he was preaching sincerity, he himself was failing in it, not in what he said, but in the way he said it. The doctrines he professed were moral, not aesthetic, and yet he chose them for their beauty. And since he didn't want to present them as beautiful, but as true, he was obliged to lie to himself about the nature of the reasons that made him adopt them. Hence such an incessant compromise of conscience that sincerely professed immoral doctrines would perhaps have been less dangerous for the integrity of the spirit than those moral doctrines where the affirmation is not absolutely sincere, being dictated by an unavowed aesthetic preference. And the sin was committed constantly, in the very choice of each explanation given of a fact, of each appreciation given of a work, in the very choice of words used - and ended up by giving the mind that indulged in it incessantly a deceptive attitude. To put the reader in a better position to judge the kind of trompe-l'œil that a page of Ruskin is for everyone, and obviously was for Ruskin himself, I'll quote one of those that I find most beautiful, and where this defect is nevertheless the most flagrant. We shall see that if beauty is in theory (i.e. in appearance, the substance of ideas was always, in a writer, appearance, and form, reality) subordinate to moral sentiment and truth, in reality truth and moral sentiment are subordinate to aesthetic sentiment, and to an aesthetic sentiment somewhat distorted by these perpetual compromises. It's about the Causes of Venice's Decadence.

"It was not in the caprice of wealth, for the pleasure of the eyes and the pride of life, that these marbles were cut in their transparent strength and that these arches were adorned with the colors of the iris. A message is in their colors that was once written in blood; and a sound in the echoes of their vaults, that will one day fill the vault of heaven: "He will come to render judgment and justice." Venice's strength was given to her as long as she remembered it; and the day of her destruction came when she had forgotten it; it came irrevocably, because she had no excuse for forgetting it. No city ever had a more glorious Bible. For the nations of the North, rough, dark sculpture filled their temples with confused, barely legible images; but for her, the art and treasures of the East had gilded every letter, illuminated every page, until the Temple-Book shone in the distance like the star of the Magi. In other cities, people's assemblies were often held in places far from any religious association, the scene of violence and upheaval; on the grass of the dangerous rampart, in the dust of the troubled street, there were deeds done, councils held for which we can find no justification, but to which we can sometimes give our forgiveness. But the sins of Venice, committed in its palace or on its piazza, were accomplished in the presence of the Bible that stood at its right hand. The walls on which the Book of the Law was written were separated by only a few inches of marble from those that protected the secrets of her councils or held captive the victims of her government. And when, in her final hours, she rejected all shame and restraint, and the great square of the city was filled with the folly of the whole earth, let us remember that her sin was all the greater for having been committed in front of the house of God where the letters of her law shone.

"The saltimbanques and masks laughed their laughter and passed on; and a silence followed them that was not without having been foretold; for in the midst of them all, through the centuries and centuries where vanities and forfeits had piled up, that white dome of St. Mark's had uttered these words in the dead ear of Venice: 'Know that for all these things God will call you to judgment'".

Now, if Ruskin had been entirely true to himself, he would not have thought that the crimes of the Venetians had been more inexcusable and more severely punished than those of other men because they possessed a church made of marble of all colors instead of a limestone cathedral, because the Doge's palace was next to Saint Mark's instead of at the other end of the city, and because in Byzantine churches the biblical text, instead of being simply depicted as in the sculpture of northern churches, is accompanied on the mosaics by letters that form a quotation from the Gospel or the prophecies. It's no less true that this passage from the Stones of Venice is of great beauty, although it's rather difficult to realize the reasons for this beauty. It seems to us to be based on something false, and we're reluctant to let ourselves go.

And yet there must be some truth in it. Strictly speaking, there is no such thing as completely false beauty, for aesthetic pleasure is precisely that which accompanies the discovery of truth. To what order of truth the vivid aesthetic pleasure we derive from reading such a page may correspond is quite difficult to say. It is itself mysterious, full of images of both beauty and religion, like that same church of San Marco, where all the figures of the Old and New Testaments appear against a backdrop of splendid darkness and changing radiance. I remember reading it for the first time in St. Mark's itself, during an hour of storm and darkness when the mosaics shone only with their own material light and an internal, earthy, ancient gold, to which the Venetian sun, which inflames even the angels of the campaniles, no longer mingled anything of its own; The emotion I felt reading that page there, among all those angels illuminated by the surrounding darkness, was very great and yet perhaps not very pure. Just as the joy of seeing the beautiful, mysterious figures was heightened, but altered by the somewhat erudite pleasure I felt in understanding the texts that appeared in Byzantine letters next to their nimbed foreheads, so the beauty of Ruskin's images was heightened and corrupted by the pride of referring to the sacred text. A kind of egotistical self-reflection is inevitable in these mingled joys of scholarship and art, where aesthetic pleasure can become more acute, but not remain as pure. And perhaps this page from The Stones of Venice was especially beautiful for giving me precisely those mixed joys that I experienced in Saint Mark's, which, like the Byzantine church, also had in the mosaic of its dazzling style in the shadows, next to its images its biblical quotation inscribed beside it. Wasn't this the case, moreover, with the mosaics of Saint Mark's, which set out to teach and made good use of their artistic beauty? Today, they give us nothing but pleasure. Yet the pleasure their didacticism gives to the scholar is selfish, and the most disinterested is still the one given to the artist by this beauty despised or ignored even by those who intended only to instruct the people and gave it to them as a bonus.

On the last page of the Amiens Bible, the phrase "if you will remember the promise made to you" is a similar example. When, again in the Amiens Bible, Ruskin ends his piece on Egypt by saying: "She was the teacher of Moses and the hostess of Christ", it's all very well for Moses' teacher: to educate, you need certain virtues. But can the fact of having been Christ's "hostess", while adding beauty to the phrase, really be taken into account in a reasoned appreciation of the qualities of the Egyptian genius?

It is with my most cherished aesthetic impressions that I have tried to wrestle here, in an attempt to push intellectual sincerity to its last and cruellest limits. Need I add that, if I make this general reservation, as it were, in the absolute, less about Ruskin's works than about the essence of their inspiration and the quality of their beauty, he is nonetheless for me one of the greatest writers of all times and all countries. I have tried to grasp in him, as in a "subject" particularly favorable to this observation, an essential infirmity of the human spirit, rather than to denounce a personal defect in Ruskin. Once the reader has fully understood what this "idolatry" consists in, he will be able to explain the excessive importance Ruskin attaches in his art studies to the letter of the works (an importance for which I have pointed out, far too summarily, another cause in the preface, see above page 100) and also this abuse of the words "irreverent", "insolent", and "difficulties we would be insolent to solve, a mystery we have not been asked to clear up" (Amiens

Bible, p. 239), "let the artist beware of the spirit of choice, it is an insolent spirit" (Modern Painters), "the apse might almost seem too large to an irreverent spectator" (Amiens Bible), etc.., etc., - and the state of mind they reveal. I was thinking of this idolatry (I was also thinking of Ruskin's pleasure in balancing his sentences in a way that seems to impose a symmetrical order on thought, rather than receiving it from it) when I said: "In what touching and tempting forms the lie may have slipped in spite of everything into the bosom of his intellectual sincerity is not for me to investigate." But on the contrary, I should have been looking for it, and would be sinning precisely in idolatry if I continued to shelter behind this essentially Ruskinian formula of respect. It's not that I don't appreciate the virtues of respect; it's the very condition of love. But it must never, where love ceases, take its place and allow us to believe without examination and admire with confidence. Indeed, Ruskin would have been the first to approve of us for not granting his writings infallible authority, since he denied it even to the Holy Scriptures. "There is no form of human language in which error has not crept in" (Amiens Bible, III, 49). But the attitude of "reverence" who thinks it "insolent to clarify a mystery" appealed to him. To put an end to idolatry, and to make sure that no misunderstanding remains between the reader and myself, I'd like to bring up here one of our most justly famous contemporaries (as different from Ruskin as it's possible to be!), but who, in his conversation, not in his books, lets this defect show, and pushes it to such an excess that it's easier for him to recognize it and show it, without having to put so much effort into magnifying it. When he speaks, he is afflicted - deliciously - with idolatry. Those who have once heard him will find his "imitation" crude, with none of its pleasantness remaining, but they will know who I mean, whom I'm taking as an example, when I tell them that he admiringly recognizes in the fabric used to drape a tragedienne, the same fabric we see on Death in Gustave Moreau's Le Jeune homme et la Mort, or in the toilette of one of his friends: "the very dress and hairstyle worn by Princess de Cadignan on the day she first saw d'Arthez. " And looking at the drapery of the tragédienne or the dress of the woman of the world, touched by the nobility of his memory, he exclaims: "C'est bien beau!" not because the fabric is beautiful, but because it is the fabric painted by Moreau or described by Balzac and is thus forever sacred... to idolaters. In her bedroom, you'll see dielytras, either alive in a vase or frescoed on the wall by her artist friends, because it's the very flower depicted at the Madeleine in Vézelay. As for an object that belonged to Baudelaire, Michelet and Hugo, he surrounds it with religious respect. I enjoy too deeply and to the point of intoxication the spiritual improvisations in which the pleasure of a particular kind that he finds in these venerations leads and inspires our idolater to want to quibble with him about it in the least.

But at the height of my pleasure, I wonder whether the incomparable conversationalist - and the listener who allows himself to be taken in - are not equally guilty of insincerity; whether, because a flower (the passion flower) bears the instruments of passion, it is sacrilegious to present it to a person of another religion, and whether the fact that a house was once inhabited by Balzac (if there is nothing left in it to tell us anything about him) makes it more beautiful. Should we really, other than as an aesthetic compliment, prefer someone because her name is Bathilde, like the heroine of Lucien Leuwen?

Mme de Cadignan's toilette is a delightful invention by Balzac, because it gives us an idea of Mme de Cadignan's art, the impression she wants to make on d'Arthez and some of her "secrets". But once stripped of the spirit within her, she is nothing more than a sign stripped of its meaning, i.e. nothing; and to continue to adore her, to the point of being ecstatic to find her in life on a woman's body, is idolatry. It's the favorite intellectual sin of artists, and one to which very few have not succumbed. Felix culpa! one is tempted to say, seeing how fruitful it has been for them in terms of charming inventions.

But at least they shouldn't succumb without a fight. There is no particular form in nature, no matter how beautiful, that is worth anything other than the infinite beauty that has become incarnate in it: not even the apple blossom, not even the pink thorn flower. My love for them is infinite, and the suffering (hay fever) caused by their proximity allows me to give them proofs of this love every spring that are not available to everyone. But even towards them, towards them who are so unliterary, who relate so little to an aesthetic tradition, who are not "the very flower there is in such and such a painting by Tintoretto", as Ruskin would say, or in such and such a drawing by Leonardo, as our contemporary would say (who revealed to us, among so many other things, of which everyone is now talking about and no one had looked at before him - the drawings of the Academy of Fine Arts in Venice), I will always guard against an exclusive cult that would attach itself in them to something other than the joy they give us, a cult in the name of which, by a selfish return on ourselves, we would make them "our" flowers, and take care to honor them by adorning our room with the works of art in which they are depicted. No, I won't find a painting more beautiful because the artist has painted a hawthorn in the foreground, even though I don't know anything more beautiful than hawthorn, because I want to be sincere and I know that the beauty of a painting doesn't depend on the things depicted in it. I won't collect hawthorn pictures. I don't worship hawthorn, I go to see it and breathe it in. I have allowed myself this brief incursion - which is in no way offensive - into the terrain of contemporary literature, because it seemed to me that the traits of idolatry incipient in Ruskin would appear clearly to the reader here, where they are magnified and all the more so because they are also differentiated there. In any case, I beg our contemporary, if he recognizes himself in this clumsy pencil, to think that it was done without malice, and that it took me, as I said, to reach the very limits of sincerity with myself, to make this reproach to Ruskin and to find this fragile part in my absolute admiration for him. Now, not only is there nothing dishonouring about sharing with Ruskin, but I could never find greater praise for this contemporary than to have addressed the same reproach to him as to Ruskin. And if I have had the discretion not to name him, I almost regret it. For, when one is admitted to Ruskin's side, even if in the attitude of a donor; and only to support his book and help to read it more closely, one is not to blame, but to be honoured.

Back to Ruskin. This idolatry, and what it sometimes mingles with the most vivid literary pleasures he gives us, I have to go down to the depths of myself to catch a trace of it, to study its character, so "used" am I to Ruskin today. But it must have often shocked me when I first loved his books, before gradually closing my eyes to their faults, as happens in all love. Loves for living creatures sometimes have a vile origin which they then purify. A man makes the acquaintance of a woman because she can help him achieve a goal alien to himself. Then, once he knows her, he loves her for herself, and unhesitatingly sacrifices to her that goal she was only meant to help him achieve. So my love for Ruskin's books was originally mingled with something self-serving, the joy of the intellectual benefit I was going to derive from them. It's true that when I first read them, feeling their power and charm, I tried not to resist them, not to argue too much with myself, because I felt that if one day the charm of Ruskin's thought spread for me over everything he had touched, in a word, if I fell completely in love with his thought, the universe would be enriched with everything I'd never known before, with Gothic cathedrals, and with how many paintings from England and Italy had not yet awakened in me that desire without which there is no true knowledge. For Ruskin's thought is not like the thought of an Emerson, for example, which is contained entirely in a book, i.e. something abstract, a pure sign of itself. The object to which a thought like Ruskin's applies, and from which it is inseparable, is not immaterial; it is scattered here and there over the surface of the earth. You have to look for it wherever you find it, in Pisa, Florence, Venice, the National

Gallery, Rouen, Amiens, in the mountains of Switzerland. Such thought, which has an object other than itself, which has been realized in space, which is no longer infinite and free thought, but limited and subjugated, which has been embodied in sculpted marble bodies, snow-capped mountains, painted faces, is perhaps less divine than pure thought. But it embellishes the universe more, or at least certain individual parts, certain named parts, of the universe, because it has touched them, and initiated us into them, obliging us, if we wish to understand them, to love them.

And so it was, indeed; the universe suddenly took on an infinite value in my eyes. And my admiration for Ruskin gave such importance to the things he had made me love, that they seemed to me to be charged with a value greater even than that of life itself. I left for Venice so that, before I died, I could approach, touch and see Ruskin's ideas on domestic architecture in the Middle Ages embodied in palaces that were failing but still standing and pink. What importance, what reality can a city as special, as localized in time, as particularized in space as Venice have in the eyes of someone who must soon leave this earth, and how could the theories of domestic architecture that I could study and verify there on living examples be of those "truths that dominate death, prevent one from fearing it, and almost make one love it"? It is the power of genius to make us love a beauty, which we feel to be more real than ourselves, in those things which in the eyes of others are as particular and as perishable as ourselves.

The poet's "Je dirai qu'ils sont beaux quand tes yeux l'ont dit" ("I'll say they're beautiful when your eyes have said so") isn't very true, if we're talking about the eyes of a beloved woman. In a certain sense, and whatever the magnificent revenge it prepares for us, even on this poetic terrain, love depoticizes nature. For the lover, the earth is no more than "the carpet of his mistress's beautiful childlike feet", nature no more than "his temple". Love, on the other hand, which leads us to discover so many profound psychological truths, closes us off to the poetic feeling of nature, because it puts us in egoistic dispositions (love is the highest degree in the scale of egoisms, but it is still egoistic) where poetic feeling is difficult to produce. Admiration for a thought, on the other hand, brings out beauty at every step, because it awakens the desire for it at every moment. Mediocre people generally believe that allowing ourselves to be guided in this way by the books we admire robs our faculty of judgment of some of its independence. "What do you care what Ruskin feels like: feel for yourself? Such an opinion is based on a psychological error that will do justice to all those who, having accepted a spiritual discipline in this way, feel that their power to understand and feel is infinitely enhanced, and their critical sense never paralyzed. We are simply in a state of grace, where all our faculties - our critical sense as well as the others - are enhanced. This voluntary servitude is the beginning of freedom. There is no better way to become aware of what we feel ourselves than to try to recreate in ourselves what a master has felt. In this profound effort, it's our own thoughts that we bring to light, along with his. We are free in life, but with goals: the fallacy of the freedom of indifference has long since been exposed. An equally naïve fallacy is obeyed by writers who unknowingly empty their minds at all times, believing they are ridding them of all external influence, to ensure they remain personal. In reality, the only cases in which we really have the full power of our mind are those in which we don't believe we're being independent, or in which we don't arbitrarily choose the goal of our effort. The novelist's subject, the poet's vision, the philosopher's truth impose themselves on them in an almost necessary way, external as it were to their thought. And it is by subjecting his mind to rendering this vision, to approaching this truth, that the artist truly becomes himself.

But when I speak of the passion I had for Ruskin's thought, which was a little fake at first, but so profound afterwards, I'm speaking with the help of memory, and a memory that remembers only the facts, "but of the deep past can grasp nothing". It is only when certain periods of our lives are closed forever, when, even in the hours when power and freedom seem given to us, we are forbidden to stealthily reopen the doors, it is when we are unable to return even for a moment to the state we were in for so long, it is only then that we refuse to let such things be abolished entirely. We can no longer sing them, for having disregarded Goethe's wise warning that there is poetry only in things we still feel. But since we can't rekindle the flames of the past, we at least want to collect its ashes. In the absence of a resurrection of which we no longer have the power, with the icy memory we have kept of these things - the memory of facts that tells us "you were such" without allowing us to become so again, that affirms to us the reality of a lost paradise instead of restoring it to us in memory - we at least want to describe it and constitute a science of it. It's when Ruskin is far from us that we translate his books and try to fix in a resembling image the traits of his thought. So you won't know the accents of our faith or our love, and it's only our piety that you'll see here and there, cold and furtive, busy, like the Theban Virgin, restoring a tomb.

Afterword by the Translator

Born on July 10, 1871 in Auteuil, France, Proust grew up in a privileged environment and trained his literary skills at the best universities. Surrounded by the best of Parisian society, Proust built a literary career in the late 19th and early 20th centuries, and to this day has a cult following of Proustian. Proust never claimed to be a philosopher and considered himself an artist, but as with most writers, his art has a distinct philosophy woven through it. He comments on other writers like Diderot throughout his works. Proust's philosophy can be characterized by his relentless pursuit of self-knowledge and the examination of subjective experience. While Socratic, it is also deeply nostalgic, emotional, and focused on the individual's subjective, hedonistic experience of life. Proust's multidisciplinary approach, incorporating elements of psychology (Freud and Jung were publish at the same time he was), philosophy, and aesthetics. He advanced French literature and his work is still a source of inspiration for artists working in various fields today.

Proust moved within the intellectual and artistic circles of Paris, associating with influential figures such as painters, writers, and musicians. His critics contend that Proust's preoccupation with elite circles failed to address the concerns and experiences of a wider range of individuals. His friendships and acquaintanceships with individuals such as Robert de Montesquiou, Reynaldo Hahn, and Jean Cocteau provided him with diverse perspectives and artistic inspiration. Throughout his life, Proust struggled with his writing and devoted immense time and effort to perfecting his prose. His commitment to literary craftsmanship and attention to detail is evident in the rich tapestry of his writings. Filled with poetic language and intricate descriptions, Proust's works challenge readers to engage with their own subjective experiences. He published few works compared to other writers of his time, but he left an indelible mark on literature with his magnum opus, In Search of Lost Time (À la recherche du temps perdu). Proust's work is characterized by his introspective exploration of memory, time, and the intricacies of human relationships.

As for Proust's own influences, he was greatly influenced by the works of writers such as John Ruskin, Charles Baudelaire, and Gustave Flaubert. These literary giants played a role in shaping Proust's style as he absorbed their insights into art, beauty, and the intricacies of human nature. Proust's voracious reading habits and intellectual curiosity allowed him to draw from a wide range of sources, enriching his own unique perspective. One of Proust's major influences was the German philosopher Friedrich Nietzsche, who explored the concept of memory and its relationship to the construction of identity. Proust echoed Nietzsche's exploration, stating, "The memory of things past is not necessarily the memory of things as they were" (*À la recherche du temps perdu*). Proust argued that this memory is subjective, as did Nietzsche and Schopenhauer. Proust explores the masks and roles imposed by society, challenging individuals to question the authenticity of their own identities and the societal expectations that shape them. Proust's writing also shows the influence of the French philosopher Henri Bergson, known for his theories of time and duration. Proust's notion of time as a fluid and non-linear entity, captured in his famous line, "The past is not simply the past, but a prism through which the subject filters and reshapes his present and future" (À la recherche du temps perdu), plagiarizes Bergson's famous phrases about the elusiveness of time.

Camusian Absurdity and Proustian Subjectivity

"I cannot read Proust without feeling that I am taking a bath in someone else's dirty water." - Albert Camus

Perhaps no philosopher hated Proust more than Camus. He began his career in Proust's shadow, publishing The Stranger in 1942, so there was naturally a bit of professional jealousy here. Camus, known for his anti-existentialist and anti-Socratic philosophy, criticized Proust's approach as excessively self-indulgent and overly concerned with introspection. Camus argued that Proust's writing lacked engagement with the outside world and failed to address the larger existential questions that he considered more relevant. Perhaps this is also a recognition that Proust's philosophy is related to Camus, and Camus had to distinguish himself from his predecessors, as both of these French authors were relativistic, Modernist and deconstructivist in their Subjectivity they both received from Nietzsche.

There are still some existentialist elements in Proust, while Camus was enthusiastically anti-existentialist and Anti-Socratic. While both are solipsistic and unable to posit a trans-personal reality in their subjectivism, Proust at least posits the possibility of knowing oneself. While his work contains elements of psychological realism, he also explores existentialist themes. The French philosopher Jean-Paul Sartre recognized this aspect when he remarked, "Proust is the novelist of the existentialists" (Jean-Paul Sartre). Proust's exploration of the self, the nature of existence, and the search for meaning are consistent with existential concerns. Proust still has an essentially Socratic view of the self, despite his hero Nietzsche's hatred of Socrates and Jesus above all other historical figures.

Like Camus, Proust emphasizes the tactile experience and sees this immediate experience of the material world as therapeutic. Central to Proust's philosophy is the concept of involuntary memory, which he describes as the unexpected resurgence of past sensations triggered by sensory stimuli. Proust believed that these fleeting moments of memory contain profound truths about ourselves and our existence. The transformative power of memory constructs our understanding of the world and enables people to grasp the intricate connections between past and present. Proust's Nietzschean subjectivity centers on the idea that our perception of reality is shaped by individual experiences, memories, and emotions. He explores the transformative power of memory, emphasizing its subjective nature and its ability to reconstruct the past throughout all of his novels. His massive 7-part novel In Search of Lost time exhibits this connectivity perfectly.

The recognition and acceptance of the absurd differs between Camus and Proust. Camus believes in confronting and rebelling against the absurd, while Proust's characters navigate the absurd by delving into the depths of their subjective experiences, finding solace and meaning in their personal narratives. An Epicurean to the core, Camus advocated the avoidance of suffering at all costs and the sacrifice of everyone and everything for one's own benefit. Proust, a bit of a Stoic, argued for the redemptive nature of suffering: "We are cured of a suffering only by experiencing it fully." Camus advocates a personal revolt against the absurd, seeing all suffering as unreal, while Proust advocates accepting the impermanence of suffering and responding with art and emotion.

Nietzsche and Proustian Subjectivity

Aesthetics is severely underdeveloped in Proust compared to his protégé Nietzsche. Nietzsche's emphasis on the resonant power of the antinomies of the Apollonian and Dionysian in the Collective Unconscious and the irrational Will-to-Power contrasts with Proust's more introspective and introspective approach to beauty. Nietzsche's evolution of Goethe's "urphänomen" emphasized the unity of different phenomena, where the individual aspects contribute to the overall beauty. Proust deviates from the field of objective Aesthetics and simply locates beauty as and individual experience rather than a communication with a universal or transcendent reality. The experience of Beauty leads Proust not to the divine, but to the sensual, a type of Epicureanism, so his Aesthetic theory is paper-thin. It is merely a way to give life a type of localized meaning, but the "only question that matters" to Camus, why live instead of commit suicide, is unanswered in Proust. In the Prisoner, Proust writes of his renunciation of Nietzsche's Aesthetics:

> I had none of the scruples of those whose duty, like Nietzsche's, dictates that, in art as in life, they flee from the beauty that tempts them, and who tear themselves away from Tristan as they deny Parsifal and, through spiritual asceticism, from mortification to mortification manage, by following the bloodiest of paths of the cross, to rise to the pure knowledge and perfect adoration of the Postillon de Longjumeau. I realized how real Wagner's work is, when I saw again those insistent, fleeting themes that visit an act, only to return, and, at times distant, drowsy, almost detached, are, at other times, while remaining vague, so urgent and so close, so internal, so organic, so visceral that it seems less like the repetition of a motif than of a neuralgia.

There is a latent Phenomenology in all his work, which can be seen as a response to the cold materialistic determinism of the intellectual systems in which he grew up. Like Camus, he sought to find meaning in a world disenchanted by the collapse of the subject-object paradigm, or as Nietzsche called it, the death of God in Europe.

Artistic Legacy

Proust was broadly read immediately, and gained notoriety in his time. The English modernist writer Virginia Woolf was highly influenced by Proust's writing style and thematic exploration- she considered Proust's work to be a major inspiration for her own novel, "To the Lighthouse." Woolf, while acknowledging Proust's genius, noted that his intricate descriptions and labyrinthine sentences could be overwhelming for readers. And certainly- his run on sentences are difficult to follow. Sometimes these are a paragraph long. She argued that his writing style impeded the narrative flow and made it challenging to navigate the core themes of his works.

The impact of Proust's literary corpus cannot be understated. His writings have gained a cult-like following, with devoted readers immersing themselves in his intricate narratives and reveling in his profound insights. One Frenchman, who died in 2023, had the symbol of the original publishing house used by Proust tattooed on his forehead, and before each meal he would stand and recite a passage from Proust. This religious-like devotion, especially in France, reflects exactly what Dostoyevsky predicted would happen in post-religious societies; new religions would always replace the old ones. Yet these new religions are even more insidious because they do not understand themselves as religions, as Dostoyevsky argues. He helped develop the religion of postmodernism, as shown by his influence on Woolf and Michel Foucault, one of the fathers of postmodern deconstructivism, which replaces logos with power as the core animating force of human reality. Foucault wrote, "Proust's work is an immense labyrinthine system in which the most insignificant details of life are sometimes given symbolic meaning."

To Look Upward is to Look Inward: Fulfillment of the Socratic Command

Proust and Camus' attempt at Self-knowledge fold in on themselves, and we end up with emotionalism, sentimentality and lyricism in a Solipsistic Tautology. The Socratic Oracle's command goes unfulfilled in Proust, as it does in Nietzsche who believed that there is no "Self" to know in the first place. Likewise Camus found the pursuit of self-awareness and self-knowledge to be the source of pain and suffering, and argues against it. Proust's contemporary Chesterton that one should know the self, but cannot through introspection "One may understand the cosmos, but never the ego; the self is more distant than any star. Thou shalt love the Lord thy God; but thou shalt not know thyself."

C.G. Jung would see a cosmic solution to this impossible task. He sees a critical development from the self-less unreflected God-image in Judaism through Clement of Alexandria, who understood the Self as a God-image with a Psychological and reflective Spirit. Clement of Alexandria wrote, "the greatest of all disciplines is to know oneself, for to know oneself is to know God". To Jung, this reality of the Self as a God-image is only realized in the individual consciousness through ritualistic living communion and relationship with the divine.

The Christian fish symbol is but one image of the Adam Secundus, who is an apotheosis of all Self-Images preceding it, for "Christ is the Archetype of the Self"- Hegel wrote posited something very close "Christ has reality as self-consciousness." Cardinal Newman understood this, writing" Conscience is the aboriginal Vicar of Christ, a prophet in its information, a monarch in its peremptoriness". In other words, Consciousness contains both objective and subjective truth; the biologically ingrained Hero Myth is not an illusion of the mind, but a precept of the truest true. He writes in Aion:

> Everything hangs together with everything else. By definition, only absolute totality contains everything in itself, and neither need nor compulsion attaches it to anything outside... Which of us can improve himself in total isolation? Even the holy anchorite who lives three days' journey off in the desert not only needs to eat and drink but finds himself utterly and terribly dependent on the ceaseless presence of God. Only absolute totality can renew itself out of itself and generate itself anew. Through this teaching the One and All, the Greatest in the guise of the Smallest, God himself in his everlasting fires [Isaiah 33:14], may be caught like a fish in the deep sea... and that by a Eucharistic act of integration (call Teoqualo, 'God-eating' by the Aztecs), and incorporated into the human body.

As Dostoevsky, a contemporary of both Nietzsche and Proust, details through intimate psychological portraiture, the Materialist, Subjectivist mind replaces the Idea of God (the transcendent point of reference and, in Christ, the Archetype of the Self) with socio-political presuppositions. And this replacement of That-Which-Is-Highest with socio-political dogma results in a "possession" of the Anima or Animus, which eradicates the individual's ability to know oneself, forever stuck in a self-same Tautology of consciousness. Jung likewise argued that Freudian Psychotherapy (which Proust was a reader of) was an important step, but lacks a relationship with something transcendent that can actually heal the νοῦς, not simply mend it enough to function:

> No amount of explaining will make the ill-formed tree grow straight... Your picture of God or your idea of Immortality is atrophied; consequently, your psychic metabolism is out of gear... experience shows that many neuroses are caused by the fact that people blind themselves to their own religious promptings because of a childish passion for rational enlightenment... A religious attitude is an element in psychic life whose importance can hardly be overrated. And it is precisely for the religious outlook that the sense of historical continuity is indispensable... what we are pleased to call [an illusion] maybe for the psyche a most important factor of life- something as indispensable as oxygen for the organism- a psychic actuality of prime importance... everything that acts is actual.

Tim Newcomb
Stuttgart, Germany
Summer 2023

Timeline of Proust's Life and Works

1871: Birth of Marcel Proust
Marcel Proust is born on July 10th in Auteuil, France, to a wealthy bourgeois family, setting the stage for his later exploration of the French aristocracy in his monumental work.

1878: Nietzsche's Major Works
Nietzsche publishes Human, All too Human (Menschliches, Allzumenschliches). Here he establishes his Perspectivism and Nietzsche begins to gain popularity in France.

1882-1889: Education and Influences
Proust attends the Lycée Condorcet in Paris, where he encounters writers including Charles-Augustin Sainte-Beuve, whose literary theories greatly influence his later work. During this time, Nietzsche was a major intellectual influence and published Thus Spoke Zarathustra in 1883.

1871: Darwinism
Charles Darwin publishes the Descent of Man, which would be followed by Origin of Species. This restoration of a Teleology to a deeply materialistic world would conflict with the Materialism of Feuerbach, Marx and suggest that life has an inherent Telos.

1895: Proust's First Publication
Proust publishes his first work, "Les Plaisirs et les Jours" (Pleasures and Days), a collection of short stories and essays, which showcases his early writing style and themes of memory and love. The same year, Freud published "The Interpretation of Dreams".

1905
Friedrich Nietzsche publishes Beyond Good and Evil, a cry to reject all types of "herd morality" and embrace the concept that Might Makes Right, paving the way for the Nazi regime and moral relativism. G.K. Chesterton publishes Heretics.

1908
G.K. Chesterton publishes Orthodoxy, responding to Nietzsche's Transhumanism and the Eugenics & Utilitarianism of Modernist writers including his friend George Bernard Shaw.

1913: Contre Sainte-Beuve

Proust completes "Contre Sainte-Beuve" (Against Sainte-Beuve), a critical essay in which he challenges traditional literary criticism and explores his own philosophy of writing and self-discovery. The same year, Franz Kafka publishes The Metamorphosis.

1908-1909: Swann's Way

The first volume of Proust's magnum opus, "À la recherche du temps perdu" (In Search of Lost Time), titled "Du côté de chez Swann" (Swann's Way), is published, introducing the reader to the themes of memory, time, and the exploration of consciousness.

1914-1918: World War I

The outbreak of World War I disrupts Proust's writing process, and he devotes himself to volunteer work and caring for wounded soldiers, while continuing to work on his novel in the evenings.

1922: Sodome et Gomorrhe

The fourth volume of "À la recherche du temps perdu," titled "Sodome et Gomorrhe" (Sodom and Gomorrah), is published, exploring themes of homosexuality, desire, and societal norms, challenging prevailing moral and social conventions.

1927: Prix Goncourt

Proust is posthumously awarded the prestigious Prix Goncourt for the final volume of "À la recherche du temps perdu," titled "Le Temps retrouvé" (Time Regained), affirming the significance and impact of his literary achievement. The same year, "Being and Time" by Martin Heidegger is published and Woolf publishes To the Lighthouse, which was inspired by In Search of Lost Time.

1931: Death of Marcel Proust

Marcel Proust passes away on November 18th in Paris, leaving behind a literary legacy that continues to captivate readers.

1947: Existentialist Philosophy

Building off Kierkegaard, Existentialist philosopher Jean-Paul Sartre publishes "Being and Nothingness," furthering existentialist thought and emphasizing the themes of subjectivity, freedom, and the individual's role in shaping their own existence, aligning with some of Proust's philosophical concerns.

1960: The Birth of Poststructuralism

French philosopher Jacques Derrida introduces the concept of "deconstruction" in his work "Writing and Difference," challenging traditional notions of meaning and truth, echoing Proust's exploration of language, perception, and the multiplicity of interpretations. This hyper-subjectivism

1980s: Proustian Revival

Proust experiences a resurgence in popularity, with scholars and readers revaluating his works and celebrating his innovative narrative techniques and profound exploration of memory, influencing the fields of literature, philosophy, and cultural studies. To this day, there are Proust literary clubs that essentially function like religions.

Glossary of Philosophic Terminology

Mémoire involontaire (Involuntary Memory)
The concept of sudden and unexpected memory recall triggered by sensory experiences, such as taste, smell, or sound. Proust delves into the profound impact of involuntary memory on human consciousness and the evocation of past emotions and experiences.
"Remembrance of things past is not necessarily the remembrance of things as they were." (À la recherche du temps perdu)

Temps perdu (Lost Time)
An overarching theme of Proust's work, referring to the irretrievability and transitory nature of time. Proust explores the ways in which the past influences the present and shapes individual identity, arguing that one should dwell in the subjective experience of time as an internal reality.

"But the great thing is not to remember, it is to live." (À la recherche du temps perdu)

Le Temps retrouvé (Time Regained)
Temporality is understood by Proust as a Phenomenological experience, not a linear reality. In the final volume of Proust's monumental work the narrator attains a deeper understanding of the nature of time and the importance of living fully in the present moment.
"The only paradise is paradise lost." (Le Temps retrouvé)

L'Amour (Love)
Love, particularly its transformative and elusive nature, is a recurring theme in Proust's work. He explores the complexities of romantic and platonic relationships, the intertwining of desire and suffering, and the power of love to shape one's perception of the world.

"Every reader, as he reads, is actually the reader of himself. The writer's work is only a kind of optical instrument he provides the reader so he can discern what he might never have seen in himself." (À la recherche du temps perdu)

La Jalousie (Jealousy)
Proust delves into the destructive and consuming nature of jealousy,

examining its impact on relationships and the individual's perception of self. He explores how jealousy can distort reality and fuel insecurity.

"We are healed from suffering only by experiencing it to the full." (La Prisonnière)

L'Art (Art)

The field of Aesthetics of pervades Proust's nostalgic and philosophic works. Proust reflects on the nature of art, its ability to capture fleeting moments, and its role in provoking involuntary memories. He explores the power of art to transcend time and evoke profound emotions.

"Every artist dips his brush in his own soul, and paints his own nature into his pictures." (À la recherche du temps)

La Transmutation des sensations (Transmutation of Sensations)

Proust examines how sensory experiences, such as taste, smell, and touch, can be transformed and elevated through the lens of memory and imagination. He explores the profound impact of these transmutations on one's perception of the world.

"Our intonations contain our history; they reflect the experience of our entire past life." (À l'ombre des jeunes filles en fleurs)

L'Identité (Identity)

Proust explores the fluidity and complexity of personal identity, examining how it is shaped by memory, experiences, and social interactions. He reflects on the ways in which individuals navigate and construct their sense of self.

"The person one loves is a world of one's own." (Sodome et Gomorrhe)

Le Regard (The Gaze)

Proust explores the significance of the gaze and its role in shaping human connections. He delves into the power dynamics, desires, and emotions that can be conveyed through the act of looking.

"The only paradise is paradise lost." (Le Côté de Guermantes)

Le Passage du Temps (The Passage of Time)
Proust reflects on the relentless passage of time and its effects on human existence. He delves into the awareness of mortality, the transience of life, and the longing for permanence and immortality.

"The real voyage of discovery consists not in seeking new landscapes, but in having new eyes." (À la recherche du temps perdu)

L'Écriture du Moi (Writing the Self)
Proust reflects on the act of writing as a means of self-exploration and self-representation. He delves into the ways in which language and narrative shape and construct the notion of the self.

"For memory's sake, I transcribe my thoughts onto paper, seeking to capture the elusive essence of my being." (Contre Sainte-Beuve)

La Compréhension des Autres (Understanding Others)
Proust emphasizes the subjective nature of human perception and the difficulty of truly comprehending the thoughts, emotions, and experiences of others. The philosopher Jean-Paul Sartre would borrow some of his language in his robust philosophy of "Otherizing" and the importance of avoiding the danger of Tribalism.

"We can never truly know another person; we can only glimpse fragments of their being." (Le Côté de Guermantes)

L'Éphémère (The Ephemeral)
Proust contemplates the transient and fleeting nature of life, emphasizing the beauty and poignancy of moments that are destined to pass. He explores the tension between the desire for permanence and the inevitability of impermanence.

"In the ephemeral lies the essence of existence, a reminder of our mortality and the urgency to embrace each passing moment." (À la recherche du temps perdu)

La Perception du Temps (Perception of Time)
Proust delves into the subjective nature of time and the ways in

which individual perception and memory shape our experience of temporality. He explores the elasticity of time and its influence on human consciousness.

"Time is not a linear progression; it is a kaleidoscope of moments, shifting and intertwining in the tapestry of existence." (Le Côté de Guermantes)

Le Rôle de l'Artiste (The Role of the Artist)

Proust reflects on the responsibilities and challenges faced by artists and the nature of art. Like Nietzsche's early Aesthetics and Schopenhauer, Art is the solution to the lack of intrinsic meaning in reality. He examines the power of art to capture the essence of human experience, provoke emotions, and challenge societal conventions.

"The artist is a mirror reflecting the complexities and contradictions of the world." (Le Côté de Guermantes)

La Mélancolie (Melancholy)

The concept of melancholy was an area of thought during Proust's lifetime. Freud wrote various papers on the subject including his 1917 Mourning and Melancholy. "Melancholy" was at that time a legitimate medical diagnosis. Proust emphasized the introspection that arises from a sense of longing, nostalgia, and the recognition of the transitory nature of life.

"Melancholy is a bittersweet reminder of the beauty and fragility of existence." (La Prisonnière)

NEWCOMB LIVRARIA
PRESS

Printed in Great Britain
by Amazon